MW01245384

Darin
Fortner

BRING

THE

JUDGEMENT

Copyright © 2015 by Darin Fortner. All rights reserved.

ISBN-13: 978-1530147939

ISBN-10: 153014793X

This is a work of fiction. Names, characters, places, and incidents are either the product of the author's imagination or are used fictitiously. Any resemblance to actual persons, living or dead, is purely coincidental.

No part of this book may be reproduced or transmitted in any form or by any means, electronic or mechanical, including photocopying, recording, or by any information storage and retrieval system, without the written permission of the Publisher, except where permitted by law.

CHAPTER ONE

Thursday, May 14, 1931

Like a shadow when it declines, I am obliged to go
away. . .

-Psalm 109:23

The ringing of the telephone echoed through the still, empty rooms of the great house like the rasping of some far-off locust, momentarily veiling the soft chanting of the sharecroppers in the fields beyond. After a short interval it was followed by the sound of shuffling footsteps as the old black servant, Mordecai, came to rap on the study door and announce the obvious.

"Telephone for you, suh."

There were two men in the study. One was hardy and weather-roughened and sour, clad in a faded work shirt and dungarees, sitting forward in a straight-backed chair with his hands dangling loosely from its arms. He glanced briefly and incuriously at the study door, for he was merely the field manager, and the servant's words were not meant for him.

The second man was seated at the secretary in an abstracted pose, one hand resting on the open ledger in front of him, a position which allowed him to turn his head slightly to the left and look out the open window or slightly to the right and speak with the field manager. He was about thirty-five, slim and spruce; his high forehead was capped by thin fawn-colored hair, and his dark brown eyes were melancholy, shadowy hollows in the midst of a sensitive, tapering face. They had just returned from a tour of the grounds, and there was a cutting of primrose tucked in the buttonhole of the coat draped over the back of his chair.

This was Major Booth Sommerlott, the first man's employer and the master of Shiloah.

"Thank you, Mordecai," he called back. "Excuse me a moment, Mr. Judson."

He rose and walked along the hallway, turned and descended a handful of steps to the niche in which he had had the house's only telephone installed. He sat down at the little table within and lifted the earpiece from where Mordecai had left it.

"Major Sommerlott speaking."

"Frank Hitchens here, Major. Hope I'm not disturbing you, but I know you were intending to pay me a visit some time this morning, and I thought I'd call and catch you before you got under way. My boy has some errands to run out in your direction, and I figured he could quite easily swing by your place and bring you along here, and drive you back out again after we've had our discussion. In that case you wouldn't have to bother with that car of yours."

Sommerlott raised one side of his mouth in a passing smile. The vehicle Hitchens was referring to was a twenty-nine-year-old Trumbull touring car, complete with right-hand drive, that he had inherited from his late father. Apart from a buckboard or two it was the only vehicle he owned; it was kept under a carpet in a shed at the rear of the property and taken out only on those rare occasions when he needed to travel into town or beyond. Since he had but two servants, and both of these elderly, such expeditions necessarily involved finding one of the sharecroppers' sons who could be spared to act as his driver, usually for the grand sum of half a dollar.

"I appreciate the gesture, Mr. Hitchens."

"Good, good. I'll let Henry know, then, and I'll see you in a little while, Major."

Sommerlott replaced the earpiece of the telephone and called to his servant. When the old man trudged into view he said,

"You don't have to get the car out after all, Mordecai. I'll be riding into town with Henry Hitchens instead."

"Yassuh."

The major returned to the study to find his field manager frowning more deeply than before.

"That was one of the shopkeepers from town, I s'pose?" When Sommerlott made no answer the man went on: "Major, I know you're just trying to do the Christian thing, but if you keep on bending over backwards every single time that lot of nigras and po' trash has a little hardship, all you're going to end up doing is breaking your neck over 'em. All you're doing now is encouraging them to go easy on themselves, and take advantage of you whenever it looks like they can get away with it. Now when your father was alive-"

Sommerlott did not resume his seat in front of the secretary, but leaned across and softly closed the ledger that lay upon it.

"It isn't your place, Mr. Judson," he said tightly, without looking up and without raising his voice a fraction of a degree, "to tell me how to run my estate. Your job is to make sure the fields of

Shiloah produce as much as they are able, and I assume you are of a mind to do everything in your power to accomplish that, as I am. Or need I remind you that your living comes from those same fields?"

Judson scowled. "No, sir, Major."

Sommerlott sighed. "Fine. We'll go over the rest of the accounts in the afternoon, when I get back from town. I trust that won't inconvenience you too much?"

"No, sir," Judson said, rising to his feet. "I'm just a employee. My time is at your disposal."

Sommerlott closed his eyes when he had gone and rubbed his fingertips across his forehead. Ezra Judson was a capable and industrious foreman, an energetic worker when circumstances called for it, but he was also narrow-minded and callous, as shot through with prejudices as any man the major had ever known. Too, he had in recent years become increasingly prone to airing his opinions at the slightest provocation. It was solely for the sake of his few good qualities, as well as his long history with the major's father, that Sommerlott endured the rest.

Roughly twenty-five minutes later a cream-colored convertible rumbled up the long driveway to the house. Sommerlott rose from the seat he had taken on the verandah, throwing his coat over his arm, and went down the wide steps to the car, passing beneath the low-hanging branches of a dogwood tree as he did so. The driver, a dark-haired young man with a flamboyant yellow-and-salmon necktie, flashed a grin and leaned across to pop open the passenger-side door.

"Climb aboard, Major."

" 'Morning, Henry," Sommerlott said as he slid into the low seat. "How are you today?"

"Just fine, sir, just fine," the boy replied, and with a clashing of gears swung the car around and accelerated toward the road.

It was a beautiful day, the sort of day that makes a man want to do nothing in particular- a day for rambling. The trees were in full foliage, and a profusion of wildflowers had sprung up along every roadway and in every meadow and unused plot of land. Their sweet scent drifted on the arms of a soft southerly breeze, hand in hand with the sound of meadowlarks and thrushes declaring their tenancy. The sky was a rich blue, with only a few clouds, smaller than a man's hand, scudding along high above.

Their conversation strayed lazily from one topic to another. A comment from the major about the way the roadster handled led to the subject of driving in general, and of trips recently taken, and before long Henry was describing in glowing terms a young woman he had met a few weeks before during a jaunt with a group of friends to the county seat. Her name was Camille, he said, she worked with her mother and aunt in a clothing shop, and she had "the most divine blue eyes you every saw."

The major smiled.

A little later he asked how Henry's father was getting along.

"He's doing fine," the boy said, "though I'll tell you, he's been busier this week than I've seen him in a long time."

"Oh? Not having difficulties with trade, I hope?"

Francis Delagarde Hitchens was a merchant, the owner of two of the stores which fronted the town square in Bishop's Hill and holder of a partial share in several others. By all appearances he was doing well for himself, well enough at least to have been able to buy his son a brand-new Jordan Speedway, the very car in which they were now riding, just six months prior.

The major had more than a polite interest in Frank Hitchens' solvency. His visit to the merchant's home that morning was for the purpose of seeing whether some arrangement could be worked out for additional credit to be extended at Hitchens' stores for the families that worked the fields at Shiloah. He had been essaying similar arrangements of late with a number of local shopkeepers; it was a necessary measure in view of the ongoing hard times, and on the other hand a cause of much criticism by his field manager.

"Not as far as I know," Henry said, and shrugged. "It's hard to tell sometimes. Father rarely discusses business with me, though you'd think he would, seeing as how I'm to take over for him at some point."

They were moving along at a fair clip now, and Sommerlott, his coat folded in his lap, was holding his hat onto his head with one hand, enjoying the feel of the wind streaming past his face.

"No, it's just that for the last couple of days he's been in and out of the house at all hours- morning, afternoon, late evening. And no, I haven't a clue what's-"

The boy stopped talking all at once as they drove into a miasma. Something large had apparently died near the road, a dog or perhaps a deer, and the foetor hung across their path in a cloud. Henry waved a hand in front of his face with a grimace. The major, coughing, clapped his hand to his nose and mouth- the hand that happened to be holding down his hat, which object promptly departed his head and tumbled away behind the car.

"Blast it!" he said. "Henry, my hat."

The young man smiled weakly and brought the car to a stop. Sommerlott climbed out and walked back to where his hat sat in mock innocence at the edge of the road. He bent down to retrieve it with a groan, for it had come to rest just where the smell was worst.

As he was straightening up two things occurred: something in the stand of trees off to his left caught his eye, and he became aware of the agitated buzzing of flies. He stepped off onto the verge to get a better look.

The thicket before him was composed mostly of pines, with smaller saplings of oak struggling up here and there, and even at this proximity was nearly impossible to see into clearly. He fumbled his handkerchief from his pocket and pressed it to his face before advancing further.

He pushed through into the thicket a few steps and stopped with a jerk. He'd been certain that he was mistaken, that the indistinct glimpse he'd gotten from the road had fooled his eye.

It hadn't.

At his feet amongst the pine needles was the body of a stout bald man in a brown tweed suit, a suit with a dark stain across the middle. A mass of bluebottle flies was clustered on his torn and discolored skin, alternately springing up and alighting in a manic sibilant dance.

Sommerlott stepped back into the open air and called to his young companion. "Henry! I need you to go on into town without me and bring the sheriff back here."

Henry opened his door and started to climb out. "What-"

"No!" Sommerlott yelled, a little more sharply. "Drive into town and get the sheriff. There's a dead body here. Go!"

When the convertible had disappeared into the distance, leaving a column of dust descending in its wake, the major returned and squatted on his heels beside the body, contemplating it pensively.

Almost half an hour passed before Henry Hitchens' car pulled up again, with two other vehicles close behind. The first was a black Dodge truck with its bed completely enclosed by a wire cage and its doors emblazoned with white stars overlaid by the word "Sheriff." The second was a Model T –also black, of course- driven by the Bishop's Hill town doctor.

The major moved forward into the sunlight. The sheriff stepped down from behind the wheel of the truck and hooked a thumb under his belt.

"Well. Major Sommerlott," he said. "And just what do we have here?"

Sheriff John M. Talmadge was a tall man, just a shade over six feet, with a rangy frame that was starting to run a bit thick around the middle. His long, sober face was set with glittering black eyes, and his thick black hair was tucked up under a flat-brimmed ranger's hat. Over his tan uniform he was wearing a brown coat; the gold star pinned to the breast pocket gleamed liquidly in the bright sunshine.

He and his two deputies were the sole police force for the bottom end of their county, which rested on the Savannah at that point where the South Carolina Low Country rises up to meet the pastoral Midlands. His jurisdiction included not only the town of Bishop's Hill but the bits and pieces around it, remnants of hamlets and villages expunged by the influenza outbreak of 1918.

Sommerlott said, "Dead body, Sheriff. And I suspect it wasn't natural causes."

Talmadge headed for the thicket, waving for the doctor to join him.

The doctor presented an interesting contrast to the lawman. Horace Van Allen was a small man and natty in every aspect, from his pinstriped navy suit to his carefully-trimmed grey hair and neat moustache, not to mention a medical bag polished to a high sheen.

"Looks like the foxes've been at him," Talmadge said, staring at the body. "What do you think, Doctor?"

Van Allen had knelt beside the body and was probing at the dead man's stomach with his fingers. "He's dead," he said, "but I reckon you knew that. Appears to have a couple of holes in him, more than likely gunshot wounds, but I couldn't say for certain until I get him back to town and on my examination table." He stood up and began slapping at his knees.

"Didn't take him long to get himself done away with, that's for certain. Always was a provoking cuss."

Talmadge turned to the major. "You recognize him?"

Sommerlott shook his head. "He looks familiar to me, but I can't seem to place him."

"That's right, you don't get into town all that often, do you? The last time you saw him was probably twelve years ago, when he still had some hair on his head. That's Perry duBree, old Lex duBree's son. He'd been in town little more than a month. Looks like somebody decided it was time for him to leave us again." The sheriff paused and gestured at his deputies. "Nate, Olin, empty his pockets and go ahead and load him on the truck. Then take a good look around just in case whoever did it decided to leave some evidence laying about and make my job easier."

He turned back to Sommerlott. "So, how did you happen across our boy here, Major?"

Sommerlott related briefly how he had come to lose his hat on that section of road.

". . .Then, when I was straightening up, I caught a glimpse of something metallic in among these trees. I thought I might have been mistaken about what I saw, but I wasn't. I walked through here and found him just the way you see him, with that gold watch dangling from his vest."

"And you could see that all the way from the road?" The sheriff rubbed his chin and considered the other man. "You've always had sharp eyesight, haven't you, Major? You were a sharpshooter in the War, isn't that right?"

"That's right."

Talmadge stepped away from the body, which his deputies were now lifting onto a large sheet. "And I s'pose you also noticed how the grass is tramped down over here by the road, as if somebody'd been marching through here not too long ago? Or did you do that?"

"No, it was that way when I got here. Though I admit I didn't notice it until after I'd sent Henry into town to fetch you."

"Mm." The sheriff crossed his arms and stared at the patch of flattened grass, thinking of the work and trouble that lay ahead of him. It had been almost ten years since there had been a murder in his end of the county, the time Job Shadduck came home blind drunk after losing his job at the textile mill across the river in Sylvania and beat his poor half-wit brother to death with a broken chair leg- and then confessed in tears to the Baptist preacher the very next morning. Talmadge had a suspicion that this time things weren't going to work out quite so easily.

"Well," he said finally, "there's no reason for me to keep you and the boy here any longer, Major. But you will be sure and stop by my office later on, won't you, so's we can get your statement down in writing? Have to make sure everything gets done just so in this sort of situation."

"Of course, Sheriff."

"Right. I appreciate it. Good day, Major."

CHAPTER TWO

Friday, May 15, 1931

By skillful direction you will carry on your war, and in the multitude of counselors there is salvation.

-Proverbs 24:6

Nate Christie dropped his boot-shod feet to the floor with a clatter and straightened up in his chair as Major Sommerlott entered the part of the courthouse set aside for the police station. The man with him on the other side of the low wooden railing, leaning comfortably against the unoccupied second desk, looked up at their visitor with undisguised interest.

The major asked, "Is Sheriff Talmadge in?"

Christie shook his head. "Sheriff's gone across to Anson's to get some lunch. You want me to have Miss Bernetta ring him up for you?"

"No, no, I can walk over and talk to him. Thank you."

Sommerlott turned toward the door. The third man said quickly, "Before you go, Major, can you spare a minute to answer a few questions?"

The deputy's caller was Marcus Raft, one and only reporter for the local newspaper. He was a short, dark fellow with a perpetual canny expression who was often to be found haunting the halls of the courthouse or passing the time with one or other of the deputies, waiting for some interesting tidbit of information to fall into his lap. For him the events of the previous day had been manna from heaven.

"I'm sure," he continued, "the townspeople would be greatly interested in hearing the impressions of the first person to find the body."

Raft was in fact one-third of the *Register*'s entire staff: his uncle, Jonas Markaby, edited the paper and contributed a few of the columns, his brother Roderick operated the pressroom and delivered the finished copies, and he had the task of filling the remaining space on its six pages with various items of local consequence.

In a town the size of Bishop's Hill, of course, that sort of family affair was hardly a rarity. Christie, for instance, was the sheriff's sister's boy, while the other deputy, Olin Anders, was the son of an old school friend.

Sommerlott paused momentarily but said only, "I've nothing to add to what the sheriff's already told you."

"Are you sure now?" Raft persisted. "You must've had some good reason for coming in here today and asking after our fine sheriff. Could it maybe have something to do with what happened yesterday?"

Sommerlott shook his head with a faint smile, and passing out of the building set off briskly across the courthouse lawn.

The southwest corner of the square was taken up by the four-story Anson McCullough Hotel, built in 1899 by a Charleston businessman and referred to by the townspeople simply as "the hotel," since it was the only one to be had for miles around. Several years ago the current owner had enlarged the hotel's dining room, adding a separate street entrance in the bargain, and it was this that was known locally as "Anson's." It was one of only two eating establishments in Bishop's Hill; the other was Kemmerfeld's

Drugstore, a block north of the courthouse, which was frequented mostly by the young people.

Sommerlott caught sight of the sheriff as soon as he entered the restaurant. Talmadge was seated at one of the window tables, a thing he preferred because it allowed him to look out over the square while he ate. With him at his table was a man by the name of Cullers, a member of the town council.

Sommerlott headed directly for their table even though the two appeared to be deep in conversation.

"Hello, Sheriff. Mr. Cullers. If it isn't an intrusion, may I join you?"

"By all means, Major," said Cullers, changing seats to make room for him. "As a matter of fact, we were just discussing-"

A soft female voice said at his right ear, "Hello, Major."

Sommerlott lifted his face to the waitress with a boyish smile. "Hello, Rose."

Rosalee Noulton was small and trim, with an unusual complexion. She had thick, naturally curly black hair that reached to between her shoulder blades (though at the moment it was pinned in a great whorl on the back of her head), hair so dark that in direct sunlight it had bluish highlights. At the same time a faint dusting of freckles lay across her cheeks and the bridge of her upturned nose, and her eyes were a light green, the color of spring apples. She was a vivacious and warm-hearted girl, with an infectious good cheer; her personality was so expansive and effervescent, in fact, that it was quite easy to forget her lack of height, and Sommerlott had on more than one occasion been startled to see her sit down and arch her feet in order to make her toes touch the floor.

She and Sommerlott had met at a cotillion a few years earlier, and despite their vastly differing backgrounds and the more than ten years' difference in their ages, through some process he still did not fully comprehend, they had become devoted friends. Even now she made sure to save at least one dance for him at every picnic and social, whether she knew for a certainty that he would be there or not.

Under other circumstances they might well have become far more than friends. Once, to tease him, she had said: "Tell me, Major, what sort of girl do you see yourself marrying? Someone tall and cool and blond, perhaps, or some spitfire redhead, or possibly even a brunette. . .?"

He had turned to her with solemn eyes and replied in a low tone, "My dearest Rose, you know if ever I were to take a wife, there is only one girl in the whole world whose hand I would ask for."

She had kissed him tenderly on the corner of his mouth and said nothing more, for she knew as well as he did that he would never marry.

"And what would you like today, Major?"

"Just coffee, please. I've already eaten."

"Black, as usual?"

"Yes, thank you." He watched her move away and turned back to his companions reluctantly. "I believe you were saying, Mr. Cullers, that you were just discussing the murder? It makes my arrival rather convenient, since that was the very subject I wanted to go into with the sheriff. I read the account in this morning's newspaper, and it seemed to me there was something missing from it, something that I wanted to ask the sheriff about."

"By all means, ask," Talmadge said.

"I know that you gave Marcus Raft a brief statement about the crime, and I suppose he gathered the rest of his information from your deputies and other people around the courthouse, as he usually does. But I wondered if there was a certain piece of evidence that you didn't mention, that you told your men to keep quiet about?"

Cullers glanced at the sheriff, whose expression betrayed nothing, and swung his gaze back to Sommerlott. "What are you talking about, Major?"

"I was thinking of the vehicle the murderer was driving," Sommerlott said, keeping his eyes on the sheriff's face. "Now it's not really any of my affair, of course, and I don't want to put my two cents in where it's not wanted, especially if I'd be telling you what you already know, but I had to be certain. . ."

"What is this? The vehicle the murderer was driving? Why didn't you mention this before, Sheriff?"

Talmadge said levelly, "Just what do you know about it, Major?"

Sommerlott shrugged and smiled briefly at Rose as she set a cup of coffee and a saucer in front of him. "Only this," he said, leaning forward and lowering his voice so that just the two of them could hear him. "I think there's a fair possibility the murderer was driving a blue automobile."

Talmadge asked, in the same neutral tone, "And what makes you say so? D'you see something yesterday you didn't tell me about?"

"I didn't point it out only because I didn't think it my place to tell you your business. . . While I was waiting for you and your deputies to arrive I took the opportunity to look over the body –purely for the sake of curiosity, you understand, and without touching anything- and one thing I noticed was that there were traces of blue paint on the buttons on his right coat sleeve. Now there's always a chance that that paint came from somewhere else entirely, but it's most likely that Perry duBree brushed up against the murderer's car at some point –or truck, or whatever it was- and those sharp brass buttons of his picked up some of its paint.

"I didn't see any reference to blue paint in this morning's paper, though, so I wanted to talk to you and find out what you knew about it."

"Is he right, Sheriff?" Cullers asked. "Was there paint on duBree's sleeve?"

Talmadge shrugged. "Tell you the truth, I haven't had time to sift through his clothes yet."

Silence settled over their table. Sommerlott, having said what he had come to say, was trying to empty his coffee cup with as much dispatch as etiquette would allow when Cullers spoke again.

"Are you very busy at Shiloah just now, Major?"

Sommerlott replaced his cup in its saucer before replying. "We started the planting of this year's crop a week or so ago, but no, I wouldn't say I'm overly busy. Why do you ask?"

"I have a suggestion to make," Cullers said, "and I beg you gentlemen to let me finish before you begin raising objections.

"The sheriff's told me about your discovery of the body, how you happened to spot a bit of metal through that stand of trees that turned out to be Perry duBree's pocket watch. And now this business about blue paint on his coat sleeve. . . If I may say so, you seem to make it a habit to notice things other men don't.

"You may not have been aware of this, but we haven't had a killing in these parts for probably a good ten years or more. A knifing or two in Wash-town come Saturday night, yes, but no murders. Now Sheriff Talmadge is a first-class lawman, I've no complaints whatsoever to make about the job he does, but the plain fact is he hasn't any experience at handling this sort of thing. It wouldn't hurt for him to have someone alongside him in this investigation, someone to make sure he didn't overlook anything.

"If you can spare the time, Major, I think that person ought to be you."

Sommerlott did not respond immediately. The sheriff cocked his head at Cullers and asked drily,

"You suggesting I should deputize him?"

"I hardly think that'll be necessary," Cullers replied, his tone matching the sheriff's. "I've no doubt the town council would be willing to pass a resolution authorizing the major to assist you in this investigation, of course, if you wanted it to be official, but we aren't talking about a permanent situation by any means. He'd only be lending you and your men a hand until you caught the killer, or until the point you decided you'd done all you could and it was time to call in the State Police –something I'd like to avoid every bit as much as you would." Cullers shrugged. "John, all I'm saying is that under the circumstances, having another pair of eyes looking over your shoulder is just good sense. How's the expression go? Two heads are better than one?

"At any rate, this is all no more than an idle fancy unless the major's willing to give us his help."

Sommerlott lifted his head from examining the inside of his empty cup. "If you think I can be of service, Sheriff, I'll give you whatever assistance I can."

Talmadge was silent for some time, but at last seemed to come to a decision. He extended his hand to the major.

"I appreciate the offer. Like Mr. Cullers says, it can't hurt any to have another point of view on the matter." He pushed his chair away from the table. "If you're free just now, Major, I'd like to start by taking you over to have a look at Perry duBree's house."

"Of course."

They crossed first to the east side of the square, where Sommerlott's car was parked in the shade of a young ash tree, and found the boy who had driven him to town drowsing behind the wheel, his small chin almost touching his breastbone. Sommerlott shook him awake gently and informed him of where they were going; whereupon the boy said, "Yassuh. I be right here, suh," and promptly fell asleep again.

As they walked away Talmadge said, "tell me something, Major- did you really come all the way into town today just to quiz me about the buttons on Perry duBree's coat?"

Sommerlott raised his eyebrows. "Oh, no. I may be a man of quaint habits, but I'm hardly likely to go to that much trouble simply to satisfy my curiosity. No, I had business I needed to attend to, and since I was already here in town I thought I'd take the opportunity to get an answer to my question."

"I see. Well now, what all did you know about Perry duBree?"

"Hardly anything, to be honest. I know that his was one of the older families in this township, and that they'd been well-to-do at one time, several generations back. Am I right in thinking that he was an only son, that the duBree line ended with him?"

"That's right. I don't s'pose it was ever what you'd call a great concern with him; far as anyone could tell he never had the slightest use for his relations. Apparently he hadn't spoken to his father in years. He moved to Columbia in '19, shortly after his mother died, and then on to Raleigh three years later. He only came back here when he learned the old man was dying of T.B., in fact he made it back just in time for the funeral. I expect he figured he was in line for some kind of inheritance, though as you say it'd been ages since the family'd had any money to speak of.

" 'Course, considering the way Lex duBree felt about banks, it's possible the old miser had a stash of money squirreled away in his house somewhere, but I don't believe that's real likely."

"Do you know if Perry duBree moved away from Bishop's Hill for any particular reason?"

"I have an idea about that now, but at the time all I knew was he'd managed to get more than one of our leading citizen's feathers in a ruffle. I was still a deputy then, under Beau Longstreet, and though there was some talk of our getting involved, far as I can recall we never did. Seems to me nobody really wanted to admit what exactly duBree'd done, let alone have it dragged out into the light for the whole wide world to see. Anyhow, he lit out for Columbia not long after, and the whole jimbang was more or less dropped."

Sommerlott waited, but the sheriff added nothing further. He asked, "Do you know what sort of work he did?"

Talmadge shook his head. "No one I've talked to seems to've had the faintest notion what it was he did for a living, if he did anything at all. Whatever the case, he doesn't appear to've had any shortage of money.

"Speaking of which, he had seventy-six dollars in his wallet when you found him. Tells me one thing, at least- whoever killed him hadn't any need nor interest in robbing him."

"Did he have anything unusual in his pockets?"

"D'you have something definite in mind?" The sheriff shook his head again. "No, nothing out of the ordinary. Pocket watch, pocketknife, monogrammed handkerchief, some pencil ends, a few cents in change. . .

"Tell you what we didn't find, though- his keys. Whoever killed him took those away with him.

"Matter of fact, the last time anybody saw Perry duBree alive was Tuesday morning, but old Crawford Gow, who lives in the house to the north of his, told me he saw our boy come in Tuesday evening, just after nightfall. After a bit more talk he admitted he couldn't see any too well in the dark, 'specially with the heavy cloud cover we had that night. All he could say for certain was it was somebody about duBree's size and height, and whoever it was went straight to the back of the house and drew the curtains 'fore turning on any lights."

"Do you think it was the murderer, searching for something?"

Talmadge shrugged. "I'll let you make up your own mind on that, but Van Allen tells me duBree had a decent-sized breakfast in him when he died, only partly digested, so he was probably killed sometime in the late morning hours, 'fore he had a chance to sit down to lunch. If that's true, it surely couldn't've been him Crawford Gow saw Tuesday evening."

"And there's no doubt he was killed on Tuesday?"

"None that I can see. Judging from the shape the body was in and the sort of weather we've been having lately, I'd say he had to be in that thicket at least two days."

"Was the doctor able to tell you anything else about how he died?"

"Only that he was shot twice in the stomach, by somebody he reckons was standing fairly close, maybe three or four feet away."

After a moment Sommerlott said, "I don't envy you the task you have ahead of you, Sheriff. There are quite a few details to be sorted out before you'll know who killed Perry duBree, and why. And to be perfectly honest, I'm not entirely convinced of how much help I can really be to you.

"By the by, whose property is the thicket where the body was hid on, anyway?"

Talmadge nodded. "That'd be the easy answer, wouldn't it? But there's nothing there. That stand of trees is on the bottom edge of some unused land belonging to an old backwoodsman name of Elias Dernin. He's in his nineties, practically senile, and watched over by a half-breed they call Mix Jennett, who's just about as moth-eaten as he is. The two of them barely knew Lex duBree or his family; they weren't aware his son had ever left Bishop's Hill, let alone moved back again.

"Tell me, Major," he asked abruptly, "you ever get any letters from Perry duBree?"

Sommerlott glanced curiously at the sheriff. "No. I'd no reason to. I hardly knew him twelve years ago, and as far as his contacting me since then. . . Well, as you saw for yourself, if I'd caught sight of him in the street I wouldn't have known him from Adam."

"Weren't you in the same regiment during the War?"

"If I'm not greatly mistaken, you can claim the same thing yourself. Nine-tenths of the doughboys in this county fought with that regiment. He and I were in different platoons, though, just as you and I were."

Talmadge said only, "Here we are."

They had come to a narrow two-story house of simple clapboard, a house which had undoubtedly seen better days. Curls of grey paint hung halfheartedly to its sides and missing tarpaper shingles made a checkerboard pattern across the roof, though a folded ladder and a patch of fresh color under one eave testified that someone had been making efforts at restoration. Encircling house and yard was a rough wooden fence with loose, skewed pickets.

Rather than heading immediately for the front gate the sheriff led Sommerlott around the side to a small shed in the same condition as the house, with the minor exception that the paint peeling from it was white instead of grey. He lifted the latch on its double doors and swung them open, releasing a faint odor of must and sawdust.

Parked in a cleared space amongst various tools and cans of questionable liquids was a green convertible, nearly new, with its shiny leather top drawn up.

"Whatever Perry duBree was doing out along Merom Road, you can lay money he didn't drive himself there," Talmadge said, pointing at the unmistakably flat right rear tire. "So far your notion about a blue automobile seems likely as any other."

Sommerlott squeezed into the shed and peered into the convertible. A light raincoat and a driving cap had been thrown across the rear seat. He moved around to the back of the car with some difficulty and pried open the trunk; all it contained was a jack and a box of tools.

"Seen all you need to here, Major? We'll take a look at the house now, then."

They walked back around and went through the front gate, across the dusty, weed-spotted yard and up the bowed wooden steps to the little porch. Talmadge reached into his pocket and drew out a key to unlock the front door.

Noticing the major's expression, he said, "No, this isn't one of duBree's keys. I had Deputy Anders run out to Wash-town yesterday afternoon and get the spare key from duBree's maid."

They stepped inside. The interior of the house presented a marked contrast to the outside: apparently the dead man had spent a good deal of time and money on furnishings in an attempt to make his home as comfortable as possible. The room where they were standing, for instance, the parlor, had an expensive carpet in the center of the floor on and around which were grouped a striped sofa, a matching armchair, and a small coffee table with an intricately-carved border. Against the left wall was a player piano, while to the right, beneath one of the room's two windows, was a roll-top desk with a padded swivel chair. Beside it was a narrow bookcase filled mostly with magazines. In the near right-hand corner of the room was a cluttered coat stand.

Sommerlott noticed almost immediately that there were no photographs propped up on the desk or the piano, and although there were one or two paintings hanging on the walls, dark rectangles on the wallpaper showed where several more pictures, probably portraits, had been removed.

"I can see what you meant," he said. "It doesn't seem as though Perry duBree had any lack of money."

"No indeed. Well now, why don't you just go on and take a good look around, Major, and let me know if anything in particular catches your attention. Me and my deputy searched this house from top to bottom yesterday, but then of course we're just a couple of small-town lawmen."

Sommerlott smiled faintly and moved around the room in silence, carefully studying everything he saw. He ran his fingers lightly over the piano as he passed it; he stood for a time in front of the bookcase and glanced over the titles of the books and magazines therein.

He stopped when he came to the corner which held the coat stand. At the base of the stand, beside one of its four feet, lay a small metallic object. He stooped and picked it up. Talmadge came around to look over his shoulder. The object in the major's hand was a gold pin in the shape of a laurel wreath encircling a pair of crossed swords and a curved crown, a wreath which bore the letters K.O.P.

"Knights of Pythias," Sommerlott said. "Do you know whether Perry duBree belonged to the Knights of Pythias?"

"I don't," Talmadge replied, "but I will. Or d'you reckon this was dropped by his killer?"

The major did not reply. Having given the pin to the sheriff, he seemed to have lost interest in it, and was now examining the hats hanging upon the stand, in particular a brown snap-brim with a loose band.

"Sheriff," he asked, "did you by any chance find a hat anywhere in the vicinity of duBree's body?"

"Come to think of it, we surely didn't. Should that mean something to me?"

Sommerlott only shrugged.

"Well, if you haven't any definite ideas yet about Perry duBree or his killer, you will in a minute. Step on over here and take a look at the contents of his desk."

Sommerlott lowered himself into the swivel chair in front of the desk as Talmadge lifted the slatted lid. The desktop was crammed full of items, as were the drawers. Sommerlott picked his way slowly through the agglomeration, unearthing a pad of cheap writing paper, an inkwell with a rubber stopper, several pens and pencils bound together with twine, envelopes, a book of postage stamps, a book of matches, a paperweight in the form of the Eiffel Tower, candlesticks- and on and on. After almost an hour he pushed the last drawer shut and shook his head.

"I have to admit," he said, "you have me at a loss, Sheriff. I can't see anything here, with the possible exception of a half-dozen letters from a cousin in Columbia, that could have any bearing on your investigation-or wait. . ."

He leaned forward and brought forth at the end of his arm a slip of paper which appeared to have been hastily folded and thrust into one of the pigeonholes in such a way as to make it nearly invisible to the casual onlooker.

"I was wondering when you'd get around to that, Major. I'd've been sorely disappointed if you'd overlooked it."

Sommerlott unfolded the paper and tilted it toward the light. The message on it was dated a few days prior and written, oddly enough, in green ink.

It read:

> Meet me behind the
> hardware store at one
> o'clock and we'll talk. I
> might be ready to give
> you the photos. Bring
> the money-all of it.
>   duBree

"I don't suppose there can be any doubt about what this means," the major said drily.

"Nary a one," said Talmadge.

CHAPTER THREE

Friday, May 15, 1931

But a certain servant girl saw him sitting by the bright fire and looked him over and said, "This man also was with him."

-Luke 22:56

The current swirled and gurgled in glittering arcs around the narrow tires of the sheriff's truck as it made its way across the sandy creek bed. Sommerlott, one arm resting against the open passenger-side window, watched tadpoles and small fishes dart away in alarm through the nearly-transparent water.

Their perusal of Perry duBree's home had yielded, after their discoveries in the parlor, little else of any real significance. Among the few items of interest were a small black revolver and a box of cartridges which the victim had kept in his bedroom bureau, tucked out of sight beneath some long underwear at the back of the bottom drawer. The pistol had not been fired recently, and by all appearances had no actual connection to the case, but its presence indicated one thing at least: whoever had murdered duBree was someone whom he had not feared in the slightest, or he would not have gone forth to meet that person unarmed.

Of all the details brought to light in the search of Perry duBree's home, however, the most telling was a small room just off the kitchen- a room originally intended for use as a pantry, to judge from its location under the stairs leading up to the bedrooms, but converted by its late owner into something quite different.

"Look in here," Talmadge had said laconically, and preceding the major into the little room had tugged on the cord hanging from its sloped ceiling. Sommerlott had squeezed in after him, and in the scarlet glow cast by a single unadorned bulb had seen that most of the shelving had been removed;

what little remained held cameras of varying shapes and sizes, flash bulbs, and film canisters. On the right, beneath a length of twine strung with clothespins, duBree had installed an abbreviated worktable, and on this rested a miniature enlarging machine and shallow trays of film developing solution, while beneath the table were several large bottles of the same fluids and a carton of photographic paper. Also resting atop the rude table was a squat lockbox, evidently taken from a tiny safe tucked away in the corner; both safe and locker stood open and empty.

"I take it this was the murderer's reason for coming here Tuesday evening," Sommerlott had said, indicating the barren lockbox.

"Appears that way," was the sheriff's reply. "He come straight on through to the back of the house here when he entered, at least according to what Crawford Gow said, as though he had a definite aim in mind. Now as to whether he found just what he was looking for in that box, on the other hand, well, that's anybody's guess. . ."

After their inspection of the dead man's home the two had returned to the square, where they sent Sommerlott's car on ahead to Shiloah and climbed into the sheriff's truck. Talmadge had wanted to interview the girl who had worked as duBree's maid that afternoon, while the major was with him, and that meant a trip out to Wash-town.

This, in turn, meant crossing the Satchee. The Satchee was a broad, slow-moving ribbon of water, more a creek than a real river, which meandered in a semicircle around Bishop's Hill on its way south to meet the Savannah. It was by no stretch of the imagination a powerful or substantial stream- at its deepest, in fact, at the point at which it joined the larger channel, it came only as high as a tall man's chest.

On the other side of the Satchee from Bishop's Hill, across Hicksham's Ford, was the settlement of Wash-town. This was the part of the township that had been set aside for black families whose members worked in the town. Not all who lived there did so, of course, but by and large blacks who rented or owned farmland were scattered on small holdings throughout the county, leaving the rest to take up residence in Wash-town. It had been incorporated around the turn of the century in a display of left-handed charity: since they clearly could not be suffered to live alongside "decent white folk," blacks who had saved enough money to purchase property had been granted bottom land along the far bank of the river, land which regularly flooded with the spring rains- hence the name.

The truck mounted that far bank now with a creak and a sway, and a right turn a few yards on brought them to Wash-town's main street. The sheriff dropped the engine down into a lower gear, and they crawled along without haste.

But for its width, there was little to distinguish this street from the rest. There were few businesses of any sort in Wash-town; from his seat Sommerlott could see a barbershop and a men's association, and at the other end of the street a lunch counter, and between these only houses. If he craned his neck he could bring the whitewashed spire of the First African Methodist Church into sight.

Down the length of the street groups of men sat on benches and porch steps, watching dully as the long hours drifted by, slack and wearisome. Some were too old or too infirm to work, but for the greater number it was simply that there was no work to be had, and no one to pay good wages for it even if it could have been found.

There were not so many idle wretches as a visitor from distant parts might have expected. In the North, particularly in the larger cities, men were standing in bread lines or hawking apples on street corners, but here the impress of the times was not so immediately evident. One reason for this was an unexpected population shift that had occurred in the last decade and a half. Scores of blacks, in many cases entire families, had deserted the area for cities such as Chicago and New York during the wartime factory boom, and again after a state-wide boll weevil infestation decimated the cotton fields in '22, with the result that in 1930, for the first time in a hundred and ten years, South Carolina had more white inhabitants than black.

Too, the plain fact was that those blacks who remained had had the least distance to fall when the crash came. They –and to be honest, the lion's share of white families in the South, as well- had been dirt poor before; they were dirt poor still. The Depression had not affected that. They carried on as they had always done, endeavoring to scrape some meager existence from the land, supplementing their diets with squirrel or 'possum or catfish when it could be had, scouring empty patches of land for field greens to make into salad- though it was also true that all four corners of the town square were now occupied by men who squatted on old crates and cried out, "Shoeshine, suh, shoeshine?" to every passerby.

Despite the general atmosphere of glumness, there were still flashes of spirit in the conversations of the men along the street, moments when their voices rose and carried through the still and shimmering air, spurtles of laughter and raillery. As the sheriff's truck rolled past, however, the jauntiness dissipated and the voices ebbed away into silence, and one by one the luster faded from their faces, leaving them as hollow and inexpressive as earthenware fragments. Only their eyes remained liquid and animate, following the black-and-white vehicle unwaveringly as it made its way down the street.

The sheriff drove approximately three blocks and turned to the left. The second house they came to in this smaller street, on Talmadge's side of the vehicle, belonged to Art Jewkes and his family.

Talmadge pulled the truck to a stop and set the brake, and the two men climbed down to the dusty, sun-baked earth.

The Jewkes residence was narrow and roughly-built, as were the houses around it, and like all the buildings in Wash-town it was in a state of semi-disrepair. This seeming neglect had little to do with its occupants' work ethic or the number of hours in a day. It was protective coloration. Black families knew well, through harsh experience, that any who dared make their home as attractive and dignified as a white family's risked having it burned down around them while they slept, at the hands of Night Riders who felt they needed to be "reminded of their place."

Talmadge stepped up onto the porch and rapped on the screen door. Voices within the house dropped sharply in volume, took on an anxious and skittish quality. A lean and gawky hound hopped onto the far end of the porch, her nails clicking on the faded boards, and trotted across to sniff around the sheriff's boots.

After long minutes a young man of about fifteen came forward into the doorway.

"How can we he'p you, Sheriff?"

"Your sister Penny at home, boy? I want to talk to her if she is."

"Yassuh. Please come in, suh."

He held open the screen door, and the two men stepped through, removing their hats as they went. Though the doors and windows all stood open the house seemed dim and airless, and it took a moment for the major's eyes to adjust from the brilliant light outside. There was a strong smell of pork and spices: evidently Mrs. Jewkes was in the middle of preparing her family's supper.

When his vision had cleared Sommerlott saw that all the children had gathered close around their mother, just as chicks or calves will do with equal instinct, so that the entire family was crowded into the doorway leading from the front room to the kitchen; and on every face, from the youngest to the oldest, was the same wariness and apprehension shown by the men they had passed in the street. The tension vibrating from them had even communicated itself to the babe cradled in Mrs. Jewkes' arms, so that he regarded the two white men with a solemn, wide-eyed expression, ready to burst into tears at the slightest provocation. It was not, of course, that the sheriff was a bad man, or that he had ever treated their family any less than fairly in his few dealings with them, but life had taught them that when the law came into the black community it could only lead to one outcome.

" 'Afternoon, Lottie," Talmadge said, and waited while the boy whispered to his mother. "I'm thinking your Art's at work just now?"

"Yassuh, Sheriff, that's so," she said after the briefest of pauses. "At Mist' Cleary's feed store. Going on twelve years now he's been working there. 'Afternoon, Major. You gen'men care fo' something cool to drink? Some water, or some lemonade, maybe?"

"That's not necessary, Lottie. This isn't a social call. Like your boy told you, I come to talk to your Penny. There someplace quiet we can sit down for a spell?"

" 'Course, Sheriff. We can sit down right here in the front room, if that's all right. It's a mite cooler in here. . . Annice, you take the baby fo' a little bit, and Tessa, you keep an eye on that stewpot fo' me. The rest of y'all go on outside and play. Y'hear me? Go on now, git!"

The front room, though cluttered with odds and ends of furniture, was otherwise decorated sparsely, with a wedding photograph of the Jewkes and another of an older couple who were most likely Mrs. Jewkes' parents, some blue glassware filled with wildflowers, and a primitive painting of a Lord Jesus who was somewhat darker than Major Sommerlott was accustomed to seeing. The furniture was secondhand for the most part, patched and reworked in multiple places, but beneath the hand-sewn quilts and throws it was worn into hills and valleys by years of use and quite comfortable. The major settled into a rocker off to one side and had a good long look at mother and daughter.

Mrs. Jewkes was on the short side, with a round body and a face etched by exposure to sun and wind. Her frizzly hair was wrapped up in a kerchief and her roughened, calloused hands plucked nervously at her faded apron. Penny Jewkes took after her father's side of the family in build: she was slim and long-limbed, with skin the color of dark caramel and an almond-shaped face that framed large seal-brown eyes. She was very pretty, and at the age of sixteen gave promise of growing into a rare beauty.

"Penny," the sheriff said, "I'm going to ask you some questions about Mr. duBree, and you just take your time and think about what I'm asking you. First of all, what all did your usual day's work for him involve?"

"I'd go in the morning," the girl said in a low, measured voice, "just after sunup, and fix him breakfas', ever' day 'cept fo' Sunday. After he had his breakfas' and gone, I took all the carpets out and beat 'em, and dusted and swep' out all the rooms. After I put all the carpets back again, 'less'n he'd tol' me different, I went ahead and made up his lunch. He most usually come home fo' lunch. Then in the afternoon I washed the lunch dishes and cleaned anything else needed cleaning, and on Fridays I did the wash fo' the week. Then I got his supper ready fo' him fo' when he come home again, and when he was done eating and the supper dishes was washed up and put away I come on home."

"How long did you work for him?"

"Been 'most a month now, since just after he come to town. I was working fo' Miss Emmeline then, Miss Emmeline Cotterell that is, but he seen me walking downtown one day and asked was I working fo' anybody, and after his second time calling on Miss Emmeline I went to cleaning fo' him and Miss Emmeline she took on my sister Tessa."

"Tessa's only home today 'cause Miss Emmeline's gone up to Orangeburg to visit her cousin," put in her mother.

Sommerlott glanced at Mrs. Jewkes with a sympathetic expression, knowing that she was ill at ease and trying to be helpful. The sheriff went on as though she hadn't spoken.

"Did Mr. duBree have any sort of schedule he kept to? I mean, did he leave his house in the morning at any certain time, or come back of an evening at a certain time?"

"Yassuh, he usually went downtown for the newspaper 'bout nine-thirty or so ever' morning of the week. He was pretty reg'lar 'bout that. But I never knowed when to 'spect him home in the evening. I just got used to fixing his supper 'bout six o'clock and keeping it warmed up fo' him best as I could."

"I see. Now you'll forgive my being indelicate, Lottie, but I have to ask this. . . He ever interfere with you?"

The girl did not answer immediately, and her mother prodded her anxiously: "Well, child, did he? Answer Mist' Talmadge. D'he put his hands on you?"

Penny Jewkes raised her head at that, and even from his corner Sommerlott could plainly see the contempt glittering coolly behind her dark eyes.

"No more'n usual," she said.

Talmadge flicked his gaze aside briefly and cleared his throat. "D'you know what Mr. duBree did for work?"

"No, suh. I know he got envelopes wit' money in 'em ever' other week, though. One of the Armstrong boys brought 'em round to the back do'."

"Which of the Armstrong boys would that be?"

The girl shrugged. "One of the younger ones. I don't know his name."

"Did Mr. duBree have any other regular visitors that you can remember?"

"Yassuh, Mist' Carr come by several times, not the garage owner but his son, and Mist' Hitchens once or twice. I can't think of nobody else."

"What about women? He ever have women to his house?"

"No, suh, leastways not while I was there."

"What did he talk about with Mr. Carr and Mr. Hitchens?"

"I don't know nothing 'bout that, suh. Mist' duBree he didn't stand fo' me to be listening in on his conversations."

"You must've had some idea, all the same. . ."

Penny shrugged again. "All I know is, him and Mist' Carr argued a consid'able amount. Truth is, it was Mist' Carr did most of the carrying on, even though Mist' duBree had hisse'f a temper too."

"And you don't know what they argued about?"

"No, suh, leastways not nothing that meant nothing to me. One time I heard Mist' duBree tell Mist' Carr, ' 'Member, Marcel, the boy has a key to the safe, and he'll open it if I give him the word, or if something was to happen to me-' I didn't hear no more'n that, 'cause he saw me listening 'round the corner and tol' me to get on back to work, and he took hold of Mist' Carr's arm and they went off into the other room to talk."

"And of course you hadn't the least notion what he meant by all that."

Penny Jewkes' forehead creased slightly at the sheriff's tone but she knew better than to let any trace of irritation show in her voice.

"Well, I figured he was talking 'bout the safe in his workroom. It was just the rest of it, what he meant by something happening to him, I didn't understand."

"So you knew about the darkroom. Did you know about the revolver he kept in his dresser drawer as well?"

"Yassuh. He showed it to me one time."

"What about this Armstrong boy? You remember Mr. duBree saying anything particular to him?"

"No, suh. I know he give him envelopes a couple times, though, envelopes wit' people's names on 'em."

"What names? Whose names?"

"I don't recollect."

"All right. When was the last time you saw Mr. duBree?"

"Tuesday morning. I come in and fixed his breakfas' same as usual, and 'bout nine o'clock I was sweeping the flo' when a gen'man in a blue car pulled up, not in front of the house but up to the shed. Mist' duBree he was out working in the shed, and he come out and talked wit' the man a spell, then he got in the car and they drove off."

The sheriff slid his eyes briefly in Sommerlott's direction but said only, "Go on."

"That was the last I ever seen of him. I went on and swep' up the rest of the house, and when it come near to being lunch time I fried him up the tail end of some ham and some biscuits. But he didn't

come home fo' lunch, and I put it all away and kep'
on wit' my cleaning. Fo' supper I cooked up a mess
of chicken and dumplings. But he didn't come home
fo' supper neither, and after a bit I reckoned he
weren't going come home 'tall that evening, and so I
put the chicken and dumplings away in the icebox
too, and made up a couple sandwiches from the ham
I'd fried earlier and wrapped 'em up in paper and put
'em in 'longside the rest of it, fo' him to have fo' his
lunch the next day. Then I went out, just 'fore it
started getting dark, and locked the do' behind me
like always. I never seen Mist' duBree no more after
that."

"This man in the blue car- d'you recognize
him?"

"No, suh. I couldn't see his face from the
dining room window, just that it was a white man."

"What make of car was it?"

"I don't know nothing 'bout cars, suh. It was
big and blue, is all I know."

The sheriff frowned and seemed on the verge
of making some retort, but before he could open his
mouth Major Sommerlott spoke up.

"Penny, when Mr. duBree went off Tuesday
morning with this visitor, was he wearing a hat?"

"Yassuh. He took one wit' him when he went
out to his shed. I s'pose he only figured on being out
there a little while, and then walking downtown or

maybe calling on somebody, only that gen'man in the blue car come by and he went wit' him instead."

"And what color was it?"

"His hat? Brown, suh, same as his suit was."

"Did he ever wear any pins or special decorations on his clothing?"

"Yassuh, he had one of them lodge pins, from a place up in Lawrenceville. He liked to wear it in his hatband."

"Of course. You say that you cleaned and swept his entire house on Tuesday, every room?"

"Yassuh, same as I did ever' day."

"The parlor, too?"

"Yassuh. . ."

"So you would have noticed anything out of the ordinary on the floor, even if it was off in the corner a ways?"

"Yassuh, I drugged ever' single one of them carpets out ever' day and swep' from wall to wall. I knew better'n to leave the least little bit of anything on them flo's, even if it wasn't no more'n a pin. Mist' duBree he'd've never let me hear the end of it if I had."

Sheriff Talmadge asked, "Now was that the last time you were in his house, on Tuesday?"

"No, suh. I went there Wednesday morning to go to work same as always, but the house was all locked up and quiet as a graveyard. I unlocked the back do' and went on inside, and called out Mist' duBree's name several times, but didn't nobody answer, and when I took a look upstairs I seen his bed hadn't even been slep' in. So I come back down to the kitchen and looked in the icebox, and sure 'nough all that food I'd put in there the day befo' was still there. I didn't see no sense in cleaning nothing if he weren't going be there, so I come back out the house, locked the do' behind me, and come on home.

"I did the same thing all over again yest'day morning, and then yest'day afternoon we heard the news 'bout him being killed."

"I see." The sheriff rose to his feet and lifted his hat from the table beside his chair. "I believe that'll be all for now. Good day, Lottie, Penny. You give your Art my regards."

The two men walked out to the sheriff's truck in silence, each one following his own train of thought. Talmadge was the first to speak, though not until they had climbed aboard and he had wrestled the gear lever into submission.

As they rounded the corner into Wash-town's main street he said briskly, "Seems to me things are starting to come together. There can't be any doubt now that lodge pin was left on Perry duBree's parlor floor after Penny Jewkes left the place on Tuesday, otherwise she'd've found it and picked it up. Put that together with Crawford Gow's story of seeing a man come in there Tuesday night. . .

"What I reckon happened is this: duBree was killed by a member of his lodge –somebody he was blackmailing, no doubt- and after he was shot and hid out of sight in that stand of trees his killer took his hat away so's nobody'd spot the lodge pin in the band if he was found and make the connection between 'em. That's why we didn't find a hat alongside duBree's body, even though he was wearing one the morning he died." Talmadge glanced at his companion, his black eyes narrowed in humor. "Thought I didn't follow your questions about his hat, didn't you? 'Course to tell the truth it's the sort of detail only a guilty mind would worry over. If I'd seen his hat laying next to his body, lodge pin and all, I wouldn't've given it a second thought.

"And then wouldn't you know after all that trouble, when he broke into duBree's house that night to carry off the blackmail photographs or whatever it was he took out of that lockbox, the killer made the mistake of dropping his own lodge pin in the parlor and gave the whole show away himself." Talmadge chuckled and shook his head. "Life's a curious thing sometimes.

"Good thing for me he did, too, 'cause it narrows the hunt down a good bit. All I have to do now is get hold of the names of Perry duBree's lodge brothers, and start searching through them 'til I find out which one of them had good reason to want to kill him, and either owns a blue car or can lay his hands on one easily."

They had reached the Satchee by then, and as the truck started down into the water Sommerlott asked, "Do you mind if I make a suggestion?"

"By all means go ahead, Major. That's what you're here for, isn't it?"

"Yes, well, all I wanted to say was this- don't be too disappointed if the lodge pin we found in Perry duBree's home doesn't mean quite what you think it means."

CHAPTER FOUR

Saturday, May 16, 1931

"Set your hearts upon it, take counsel and speak."

-Judges 19:30

As the gateposts of Shiloah came into view John Talmadge realized to his surprise that he was whistling tunelessly under his breath. It was not that he was a habitually dour man, but he took his responsibilities seriously and felt himself a little too old for pointless frivolity, and this lightheartedness had stolen upon him entirely out of the blue. Certainly he was not here in the countryside, behind the wheel of his official truck, for a leisurely joy ride.

Admittedly, though, out here away from town it was easy to relax and let his mind wander from the task at hand. Nowhere around him was there the slightest indication that anything the least bit memorable or out of the ordinary had occurred in the last few days. That oft-celebrated amaranthine quality still mantled the landscape, still lingered in the soft dusty sunshine and gently outlined the patchwork fields. The hours and minutes seemed to move as slowly as spilled molasses, and with as little effect. The trees along the road's edge were the same trees as a week before; the grass and flowers and brush grew on unchanged. Clots of bright white cotton wool still hung in a watercolor sky, bees still murmured in the honeysuckle and birds still chirruped busily in their leafy garrets. The kudzu-vine still clambered insidiously up every post and telephone pole in sight.

In town, of course, the opposite was true- to a degree. The sudden demise of Perry duBree was the most novel and exciting thing to have happened in Bishop's Hill for a good long while, and by now it was the prime topic of conversation in every quarter, from the men sipping Cokes on the post office steps to the women flitting in and out of the dressmaker's shop to the teenagers clustered around the drugstore soda fountain, but as far as the sheriff could tell that was all that it was. No one appeared particularly put out or distressed by his death: in fact, more than one person Talmadge had spoken to had said "good riddance" in so many words. Perry duBree had possessed, it seemed, a positive talent for making himself disliked. In the final tally all his death meant for most of the townspeople was an excuse to set the wheels of the gossip mill turning, to cast a jaundiced eye on their neighbors and make some not-quite-slanderous insinuations about one another; while to the younger folk it was a puzzle on their doorstep which gave them the chance to play at being Sherlock Holmes or Nick Carter.

All of which was only to be expected, Talmadge supposed, but he was beginning to find it difficult to take five steps without being cornered by someone wanting to know how the investigation was faring or itching to share a pet theory about the killer's identity.

The only persons he had not heard from so far, in fact, were those individuals whose opinion truly mattered. As an elected official he was necessarily responsible to the people of the township, which at times meant listening to foolish questions and proposals with patience and a firmly-restrained tongue, but more importantly he had to answer to the members of the town council- the men who owned the bank and the insurance agency and the stores, who employed the greater part of their half of the county in one way or another, who held the mortgages on the farms and the loans on the automobiles, who bought the produce come market day and collected the taxes come spring; and who saw to it that he stayed in office when election time rolled around.

So far, however, apart from a polite inquiry whenever he chanced to meet one of them on the street, the council members had been entirely silent on the subject of the murder. Talmadge assumed that this silence was due, at least in part, to Lucas Cullers' conceit of having Major Sommerlott offer a hand in assistance.

Whatever the case, the result was that he was free to get on with his job, and that was exactly what he meant to do. He had no doubt whatsoever that he and his deputies would find the killer of Perry duBree without any help, given enough time, but Cullers and the rest of them seemed reassured by having someone of the major's intelligence and discretion involved, and it wasn't his place to argue the point. At least Sommerlott had shown no inclination toward trying to take over the investigation.

He swung the long truck between stone columns topped by replicas of Grecian urns and entered the estate.

Like most of the townspeople, he had been here only a handful of times in his life, and so his image of it tended to waver between memory and imagination. When he had seen it the previous evening, edged with gold by the warm rays of sunset as they slanted across the newly-planted fields, he had thought it unchanged from the faded seasons of his boyhood. Now in the stark light of midday he saw that he had been mistaken. An air of stillness hung over the grounds, particularly the main house and the long lawn leading up to it, and more than a stillness, an ossification, even a sense of something forgotten, as though the river of time that flowed so gradually onward all around had cast this place up upon a sand bar, forlorn and desolate.

Before him the main avenue –little more than a set of wheel tracks through the grass, so scarcely-travelled was it- ran along one side of the gently-rolling lawn up to the great house, passing beneath a line of ancient white elms, massive and gnarled, whose Spanish-moss-draped branches swayed sluggishly in the breeze. About halfway along the lane diverged, and a second drive passed around the row of elms, running back to the estate's outbuildings and then curving across to meager wood-and-clay cabins that had once quartered slaves but now held families of sharecroppers.

Above all of it loomed the house. It was a great brooding hulk of pale greyish-white stone, the color of a faded sepulcher, with dark, narrow windows. A verandah with convex pillars stretched across the front of the building and back along its left side. It was a solemn, mournful structure, and even with the sun glistening down from a speckled sky the light seemed muted here, diffused somehow. Three sides of it were buried beneath an impenetrable mass of ivy at which the major's manservant was often to be seen cutting, fighting with billhook and ladder the plant's encroachment upon the house's face.

As moldering and time-burdened as it seemed, however, this was not the original residence. That structure, greatly expanded and embellished through the years, had been burnt to the ground in 1865 by Yankee soldiers marching north to meet up with General Grant's troops in Virginia; all that was left remaining after the conflagration, it was said, were the extensive cellars in which the family, having heard news of the advancing Northern host, had hidden whatever valuables and pieces of furniture could be quickly and easily carried to safety. The following year the major's grandfather, Colonel Thaddaeus Sommerlott, had had the present house built in its stead, and perhaps in some alchemic way the bitterness and heartache of that season had seeped into the stones and mortar as they were set in place, for from its very beginning it had had a gloomy and lowering appearance.

Talmadge drove up the long avenue and parked in the curve of it, and then paused, half-unconsciously, to straighten his necktie and adjust his hat before starting up the walk toward the house. As he passed under the dogwood branches that arched over the path, however, the crown of his hat brushed against one and a scattering of white blossoms fell upon the brim and across his shoulders. He pawed irritably at them as he mounted the steps to the verandah and was still picking petals from his coat when he rang the bell.

It was of course Sommerlott's old black steward who opened the door, when it at last opened. Of the great cloud of domestics Talmadge recalled from his few boyhood visits, all that now remained to look after the estate were this aged and venerable retainer, Mordecai Sowers, and his equally ancient wife Hecate.

" 'Morning, Sheriff," he said, with no trace of surprise on his lined face at this unexpected visit. "The major is in the dining room. If you'll come this way, please?... Your hat, suh…"

Neither the occasional talk he had heard about the major's solitary existence here at Shiloah nor the leaden atmosphere that hovered over the estate had quite prepared Talmadge for the interior of the great house. He followed the white-headed servant down a central hallway illuminated only by two long tapers, one halfway along the passage and one at the far end of it, which served more to emphasize the semidarkness around them than to dispel it. On either side wide doorways opened onto shadowy, cavernous rooms made more so by a scarcity of furnishings.

Upon inheriting the estate and finding himself faced with the task of maintaining an enormous, rambling mansion with only a pair of elderly servants at his command, the major had had the carpets and the majority of the furniture removed to two upstairs storerooms, leaving a handful of pieces marooned and lonely amid a vast expanse of hardwood floor. At every window heavy curtains were drawn, and remained drawn all the year round, morning or evening, winter or summer- though as they went Talmadge caught here and there glints of bright light where their edges had not been brought entirely together, light which nevertheless failed to penetrate the obscured chambers. High up on the otherwise unadorned walls he could make out dim and dusty portraits of quaintly-garbed ancestors, their faces barely visible and their dreams and hopes long withered away. The sheriff did not consider himself a particularly imaginative man, but even he would have had little trouble peopling the benighted corners of this house with ghostly whispers and the rustling of phantom skirts.

There had been a time, when the major's parents were alive, when all this was not so; when the house, despite its grim and forbidding façade, had been as natural and healthy a place as any other. Shortly after they were married, for instance, the Sommerlotts had begun organizing dances and revels for the youth of the district at regular times throughout the year- at first primarily to please the young bride, who was more than a dozen years her husband's junior, by surrounding her with those her own age, and then later, after their son was born, to provide the boy with the sort of companionship that an only child would otherwise have lacked. On such occasions light and music and gaiety had filled the rooms of Shiloah late into the evening.

Talmadge found himself, as he peered past the servant's shoulder into the murk, trying to roll back the curtain of years and see his surroundings as they had once been. He had reached the point of attempting to name the rooms to which the doorways on either side led when abruptly, amidst a stream of incomplete, shifting memories, there came vividly into his mind an experience he had not thought about in over thirty years: that of standing spellbound in the salon of the great house, his mouth hanging open, listening to Genevieve Haring sing "Beautiful Dreamer." He had been eleven and she a year older, the first girl for whom he had ever had a real infatuation, and watching her stand there, tall and slim in a stiff new linsey-woolsey dress of midnight blue, her hair falling in heavy golden curls upon her shoulders and her high, sweet voice filling the room, he had imagined that that must have been what it was like when an angel from heaven came to you. . .

All things fade, however, and all things come to an end. In 1916, shortly after the start of his second year at Winthrop College in Rock Hill, Booth Sommerlott's mother took sick with blackwater fever and died. Her death was as tragic as it was unexpected, the sudden swift cutting down of a flower in the full bloom of its vigor and loveliness. Although it came as a stunning blow to both father and son, it was the elder Sommerlott who was most stricken by it. In the weeks after her funeral he seemed to gradually crumple in on himself. Thought he remained courteous and civic, a Southern gentleman to the tips of his shoes, his manner grew dry and distant, even unfocussed at times. He began to be seen in town less and less frequently. He dismissed most of his servants and ceased receiving visitors at Shiloah, instead spending much of his days hunting on the far wooded fringes of his property in the company of his adjutant, Judson, into whose hands he abandoned the keeping of his house and fields.

It was a sad and pitiable, if understandable, state of affairs; what no one could have foreseen was that before too many more years, through a longer and more tortuous chain of circumstances, the son would come to arrive at the same sort of twilight existence.

When the United States entered the Great War the following spring, Booth Sommerlott threw over his academic pursuits and enlisted. He and his fellow doughboys were shipped to the battlefields of the

Marne, to an experience for which nothing could have adequately prepared them. The conflict was a brutal one on every front, but that arm of it fought on the soil of Europe was by that point no less than hellish slaughter and carnage, a monstrous abattoir into which men were poured by the tens of thousands, a phantasmagoria played out across a surreal outer-space landscape.

In short, it was deliberate orchestrated insanity, difficult enough for a simple country boy like John Talmadge to face and live through, and many a man of more sensitive temperament came away from it shattered inside, shaken apart at the marrow in a way that was just as abiding as the physical traumas suffered by his comrades. Booth Sommerlott, now bearing the rank of major, returned home in 1919 a changed man, pensive and retiring, his dark eyes melted into shadowy pools. And yet there was more to his metamorphosis than his combat experiences alone. Though he never referred to the matter except by the most oblique of allusions, it seemed he had suffered some painful personal incident during his time "over there," some tragic episode (involving the death of a young French girl, or so it was rumored) which had sundered him from his fellow men and left a dark weal upon his soul.

As though he had not seen enough misfortune in his young life, fate had prepared a further sting for him. Within six months of his homecoming he was to bury his father, a victim of the Spanish influenza epidemic which came riding directly on the heels of the War. Thenceforward the major was alone at Shiloah, the last of the Sommerlotts, and all the weight of responsibility and tradition and community expectation rested squarely on his shoulders.

Mordecai turned as they neared the end of the hall and entered a doorway to the right, announcing as he did: "Sheriff's here to see you, suh."

Talmadge followed the old man into what proved to be the dining room. It was located at the center of the house, with the result that it could not be reached by any light from the outside. The only illumination came from a series of lamps flickering along the two longer walls, alternating with heavy curtains of deep crimson which were meant to give the illusion of windows. A narrow table of wood so dark as to appear practically black ran nearly the entire length of the room; at one end of it were positioned a few bits of china and cutlery.

Major Sommerlott had apparently entered the dining room at the instant the sheriff had rung his doorbell, for he was standing just beyond the end of the table, fiddling with his cuff links. Even on an occasion like this, for a solitary meal at home, the major was dressed meticulously, with a starched white shirt and a patterned navy bowtie; only the absence of a dinner jacket showed that he had begun to let the conventions slip.

More than ten years had now passed since his father's death, and he remained secluded and unmarried. Most of the townspeople had assumed that he would seek a wife as soon as possible, among other reasons to fill the great house with sound and vitality once more, and fell to waspish murmuring when he failed to do so. Particularly had his singleness become a subject of comment of late, in view of his unmistakable attachment to Rosalee Noulton. When the two of them turned their faces toward each other even a complete stranger could read plainly his deep affection for her, and hers for him, and yet as far as anyone knew he had never once proposed to her, or even formally courted her. Instead he continued as he was, haunting the time-shrouded rooms of Shiloah, busying himself with executive tasks during the day and musing late into the night "over many a quaint and curious volume of forgotten lore."

He extended his hand and shook his visitor's firmly. "Ah. Sheriff. Welcome. I was just about to sit down to an early lunch. Won't you join me? I assume you haven't eaten yet. Mordecai, set an additional place for the sheriff."

"Yassuh."

The meal that was set in front of the two men was of basic, down-to-earth fare, but the cook had prepared enough of it to feed a score or more: rabbit stew larded with thick pieces of carrot and potato, sour milk cornbread, collards soaked in ice-cold salt water, slow-baked sweet potatoes. . . As his manservant entered bearing a dusty bottle beneath one arm and a pair of stemmed glasses in the opposite hand the major said,

"I don't imagine you're much of a wine drinker, Sheriff. Do we have any near-beer in the house, Mordecai?"

"No, suh, I'm 'fraid not."

Sommerlott turned to his guest apologetically. "I drink little in the way of beer myself, you see, and of course with this Prohibition- well, to speak frankly, the sort of swill I could lay my hands on legally isn't worth having. . . I can offer you some freshly-made tea, however, or I can have Hecate stir up some lemonade, or" –he tilted his head toward the pitcher in the center of the table- "there's always water. . ."

"Tea'll be fine, Major."

"Now," his host said after a glass of dark tea had been placed before the sheriff, "has there been some new development in your investigation? I take it you didn't come all this way simply to pass the time."

Talmadge shrugged. "You heard what Lucas Cullers said. I'm s'posed to keep you informed of everything I do, so's you can tell me in case I happen to overlook anything. I figured I'd drive out and fill you in on what all I've done and found out, and see if you had any suggestions you cared to make."

Sommerlott said only, "Ah."

Southern tact and hospitality prevented him from pointing out that if that was the only reason for the sheriff's visit, it would have been more sensible for him to have telephoned; and for this Talmadge was grateful. The unvarnished truth was that the sheriff's presence was due less to any sense of diligence in following the town council's instructions than to an urge to briefly escape the confines of his office, and even more, though he would have been loath to admit it aloud, to basic human curiosity (or as he put it to himself, "plain cussed nosiness"): the desire to see once again a place he had not seen in many years, and to confirm with his own eyes the rumors of the major's eremitical existence there at Shiloah. Such an admission would hardly have been complimentary to either of them.

"To begin with, far as the body's concerned there's little you haven't already heard. Van Allen dug the two bullets that killed duBree out of his stomach, but there's not much I'm going to be able to do with them. The nearest crime laboratory I know of's a small one they have there in the State Police post at the county seat, and I'd probably have to bring them in on this to get access to it.

"I tried to get the doctor to say one way or another whether duBree was killed where he was found, but he won't commit himself. Personally I'm inclined to think he was killed there along that stretch of road, not shot somewhere else and brought there afterward, but I'll be hanged if I can see that that gets me anywhere."

"It makes sense, though. Perry duBree was alive when he climbed into that blue automobile Tuesday morning, and in a town as small as Bishop's Hill I'd imagine it would be nearly impossible to kill a man and dispose of his body without any number of people being aware of it- especially shot as he was. Much safer to drive him out into the countryside and murder him there."

Talmadge nodded and reached for another piece of cornbread. "I spent most of the morning tramping back and forth across the square, trying to chase down duBree's personal affairs, and there's not much there either. He hadn't any kind of a bank account –like father, like son- and far as Bernard Davenport knows he hadn't anything in the way of a will or such. I put a call through to duBree's cousin in Columbia as well, and he told me pretty much the same thing."

Bernard Davenport was the township lawyer, the man who handled any and all legal business for the people of Bishop's Hill and the surrounding area, which at times led to a rather varied practice: he might be defending a client in court against a charge of chicken stealing one week and advising the town's merchants on some fine point of investment law the next.

"I've also been 'round to Anson's, and the drugstore, and the pool hall, and the garage, and any other place a man might stop in for a few minutes during the course of a day. It was a long shot, but I thought if duBree'd stopped in somewhere the morning he was killed, somebody might've remembered seeing someone with him, some stranger- in other words, his killer. No such luck. No one I talked to recalled seeing Perry duBree around town Tuesday morning.

"Now on the other hand I did learn he'd been into Anson's only a few times since he moved back here- just enough to wear his welcome thin, apparently. Your sweetheart tells me he got into arguments at least twice with other customers. Not over anything serious, mind you, just him making a jackass of himself, and of course nobody can quite recollect who it was he'd had words with."

Sommerlott smiled faintly at the reference to Rosalee Noulton but made no comment.

"I don't s'pose duBree's little agitations are really too important, else I'd've heard about them before now, but all the same I'll keep after the folks at Anson's, in case something stirs up a useful memory. In the meantime I've got plenty of other leads to follow up.

"For instance, while I was in Davenport's office I asked him to dig around discreetly for me and find out the names of Perry duBree's lodge brothers.

I'll ask the mayor for the same favor the next time I
see him, and though he won't be too all-fired keen on
the idea I don't doubt he'll come through in the end,
and that way I'll have that part of the investigation
covered. Between the two of them they've got enough
connections to turn up exactly what I want to know.
The closest K. of P. lodge is the one in Lawrenceville,
the one duBree belonged to, and I'll bet you anything
you like that's where the man who dropped that lodge
pin is enrolled. 'Course there's a chance duBree was a
member of a chapter up in Raleigh before he moved
back here, and that's where his killer came from, but
in that case why wait 'til now to kill him?

"I got on the 'phone with the town deputy in
Lawrenceville, too, and asked him to put together a
list of blue automobiles registered in his part of the
county. Then, when I have that list in front of me, I
can check it against the list of duBree's lodge
brothers and narrow my search down a good sight.
'Course I also have one of my deputies making a list
of blue automobiles in our neck of the woods, just to
be thorough, but I find it real doubtful the killer's
someone from here in Bishop's Hill."

Talmadge glanced at his host, and seeing the
unspoken opinion reflected in his face added gruffly:
"It isn't wishful thinking makes me say that, Major,
don't believe that for a minute. I'll do my job no
matter which way the evidence points. But somehow
I can't picture a man setting out to commit a murder

in his own hometown and pulling up to his victim's house in broad daylight, in his own car, in plain sight of all his neighbors, the way Perry duBree's killer did. No, seems to me the man I'm after's a stranger here, someone who isn't worried too over much about letting his car be seen."

"There are," the major said mildly, "at least two other possibilities that spring to mind, but I'll let that pass for now. When your deputy finishes compiling his list of automobiles, would it be too much trouble to have him make a copy for me?"

The sheriff narrowed his eyes. "Don't tell me you have an idea about the killer's identity already."

"Oh, no. Nothing so concrete. I have only the vaguest of notions at this point."

"Hm. Oh, yes, I paid a visit to Frank Hitchens, as well. He had little enough to tell me. He went to Perry duBree's house once or twice to discuss some business with him, but that was all. He couldn't recall seeing anyone 'round duBree's place the few times he was there, townsfolk or otherwise, and he certainly hasn't the least idea who'd've wanted to kill him."

"And," Sommerlott said slowly, "you don't think he might be a suspect?"

Talmadge laughed sharply. "Frank Hitchens? What on earth would Perry duBree have been blackmailing him over? He's one of the whitest men you or I know. Besides, he isn't a K. of P. lodge brother, or a member of any other lodge or order. I happen to know that for a fact."

He put down his fork as Mordecai cleared away their empty dishes, returning a few minutes later with dessert on his silver serving tray, deep bowls of hot apricot cobbler covered with heavy cream.

"Well, if that don't look downright delicious. . . Anyhow, soon's I leave here I plan on questioning Marcel Carr, and then I'll stop by the Armstrong farm and try and get a line on who else duBree might've been blackmailing." He lifted a spoonful of syrupy apricot and ginger-coated crust toward his mouth. "Unless, of course, you have a better idea?"

After a short pause his host responded with a question of his own, one which seemed to have no connection to the conversation thus far.

"Have you ever heard the story of how this estate got its name?" Talmadge shook his head wordlessly. "To be perfectly frank, it's not a particularly colorful story. When the very first Sommerlott arrived in this part of the country in 1732, his Dutch-born wife by his side, they discovered that the property deeded to them by the British crown was bisected by a tiny spring-fed creek which ran –and still runs today, in fact- in roughly a straight line for more than a mile before finally swinging around to converge with the Satchee. It was so small a stream that not one of the Indian tribes who lived in the area had ever even bothered to give it a proper name. to my ancestor, however, who it seems must have been a keen reader of the Good Book, this little creek called to mind 'the waters of the Shiloah that goeth gently,' as mentioned by Isaiah the son of Amoz, and thus, from that rather obscure passage of Scripture, he derived the name of both stream and estate.

"My point, long-winded as it was, is simply that what is insignificant to one person may be full of significance to another. Although I agree with you that the blackmail angle is most likely the key to this murder, it would be wise not to overlook any aspect of Perry duBree's life. There's always the possibility that the murderer was driven by another motive entirely."

Talmadge shook his head again as a telephone rang not far off. "Believe me, I'm not overlooking anything. It even crossed my mind at one point that maybe Penny Jewkes had something to do with duBree's death. After all, she's the only one so far who's mentioned seeing a man in a blue car Tuesday morning. His neighbors remember him working in his shed, all right, but no one I've talked to seems to've noticed any mysterious visitor.

"So I put it to myself: what if her young man happened to drop 'round unexpectedly to Perry duBree's back door Tuesday morning –a girl her age, as fine-looking as she is, is bound to have a steady boy, if not half a dozen- just happening to be carrying a pistol on him, and finds duBree forcing his attentions on his sweetheart, like it sounds like he was in the habit of doing, and decides to put a couple of slugs in his belly by way of pointing out his objections? It would've had to've been the boy's doing, of course; if Penny'd killed duBree, I think she'd been far more likely to take a carving knife to him, not shoot him. And then the two of them get rid of the body, clean up any mess, and concoct this story about him going off with a man in a blue car- probably some visitor from earlier in the week, which would explain the paint on his coat buttons."

Talmadge twisted one corner of his mouth up in a wry expression. " 'Course once you stop and look at it, it all falls apart like a house of cards. If that was really how Perry duBree died, you can just bet they'd've left his body where it fell and lit straight out of town, not taken the time and trouble to haul it out into the countryside and hide it. And if for who knows what reason they did decide to do something like that, how? Penny Jewkes hasn't a car, and chances are her beau doesn't either. Not to mention that there's no way on God's good green earth duBree's neighbors could've missed the sound of the gunshots and the sight of the two of them carrying a white man's dead body out of his own home. No, it's too-"

The major's old manservant came shambling into the room at a faster clip than he had left it.

"Telephone for you, Sheriff. 'S urgent."

Talmadge frowned and dropped his spoon into the empty bowl in front of him. He followed the old man out through the door directly behind the major and into the rear hall, which led to the telephone niche.

He was back within a scant few minutes, his long face grim.

"Tell your man to fetch my hat, Major, and yours too. There's been a shooting at the Armstrong place."

CHAPTER FIVE

Saturday, May 16, 1931

I will bring upon them, upon. . . young man, the
despoiler at midday.

-Jeremiah 15:8

      Talmadge leaned on the horn yet again, and
this time the crowd drew back enough for him to pull
the truck into the Armstrongs' front yard and set the
brake.

      The Armstrong family lived on the northern
edge of Bishop's Hill, along a built-up section of

county road that the town council had been trying in vain for the last fifteen years to convince their fellow citizens to call Leaman Street. At the moment the small patch of yard in front of their home was overrun by a mass of people that spilled out across the road and up to the edge of the field beyond.

The sheriff stepped down from his truck and Major Sommerlott followed.

A crowd is a curious thing, like silt suspended in river water. No matter the scope of the incident which draws it together, unless there is some periodic agitation, some fresh excitement, it will begin to settle, to pull apart into separate elements. The crowd gathered in front of the Armstrong home had started to do exactly that, drawing away into compact knots divided by gender and social standing, whilst the younger children, quickly tiring of waiting for something to occur, had reverted to chasing one another in and out through the throng with whoops and hollers.

With the sheriff's advent, however, the crowd began to converge again, slowly at first but more rapidly by degrees as a rising electricity flickered from one to another, so that within minutes Talmadge found himself at the center of a crush of aggrieved townsfolk, the greater number of whom were clamoring for his attention at the top of their voices.

Sommerlott, left more or less in peace, took the opportunity to survey his surroundings. The home before him was a two-story farmhouse, white with red trim. It was a large structure, and every inch of it, from its basement to the attic rooms tucked beneath its steeply-pitched roof, was put to use: the household included Emory and Doris Armstrong, their six sons and two daughters, his parents, her mother, and his ne'er-do-well brother, as well as an occasional cousin or two. In front of the house was a small vegetable garden enclosed by a rough picket fence. Behind and slightly to one side of the farmhouse were several squat outbuildings in a rough semicircle, while immediately to the right was a massive weatherworn barn, all of them painted a dark red. Dr. Van Allen's black Ford was parked in the open space between them, but the doctor himself was nowhere in sight, nor were any members of the family that the major could recognize- though on the other hand a good quarter of the people he did see, if not more, were indirectly related to the Armstrongs in some way.

A figure in tan was pushing his way through the crowd, muttering, " 'Scuse me, tolks, 'scuse me," and Major Sommerlott moved around the truck to the sheriff's side. It was Deputy Christie. He started speaking as soon as he was close enough to be heard.

"It's Mattie Armstrong, Sheriff. Someone shot him from behind while he was in the garden there. They've taken him into the house, and the doc's with him now."

"The boy say anything about what happened?"

"Not that I could hear. He was moaning a bit – the shock, I s'pose- but no words I could make out."

"Anybody else see the shooting?"

"I don't rightly know, Sheriff. Between helping them get the boy inside and calling you and seeing the crowd didn't trample all over the garden and ruin any evidence there might be, I haven't had much chance to ask who saw what. I did find this, though-"

He held out his handkerchief. In the middle of the blue-and-white checkered cloth was a small lump of lead, flattened on one end and smeared with blood and dirt.

"Found it in the garden, among the cabbage leaves. Must've passed clean through him."

"Right. Fold that back up and put it in your pocket –and make good and sure you don't lose it- and then go ahead and start questioning folks. Find out if anybody here saw anything, anything at all. If they did, tell them not to go wandering off, I want to have a word with them. If they didn't, send them on home, and then when you're finished you can head back to the courthouse. I'm going inside and see how the boy's doing."

Talmadge turned away from his deputy toward the farmhouse door, steadfastly ignoring the crowd pressing in on him, and almost walked directly into Marcus Raft. The reporter's small eyes were bright.

"Well, Sheriff, what do you have to say about this latest attack? Is it tied in to the killing of Perry duBree some way? If not, what do you think's behind it? And who?"

"Not now, Raft!" Talmadge growled, and shouldered past him.

Inside the house the atmosphere, though more restrained, was no less tense. The family was gathered in the front hallway, their faces stony with fear and anger, talking in hushed voices and casting repeated glances at the stairs leading to the upper floor, listening with taut nerves for the slightest sound from above.

"What's going on in this town, Sheriff? Here my boy is shot down like some-"

"Your voice, Emory," fretted his wife.

"-Like a dog not five feet from our door!" he continued, in a quieter tone but at the same harassed pace. "Why? For God's sake, why? Who would want to do this to us?"

Talmadge caught hold of the man's arm. "Believe me, Emory, that's exactly what I intend to find out. I will get to the bottom of all this, I give you my word on that. How is the boy?"

"We don't know," said his mother, "we just don't know. The doctor's with him now, and all we can do is wait and pray. Oh, Sheriff, he was so pale. . ."

"Now, Mrs. Armstrong, you know well as I do it'll do none of us any good to imagine the worst. The best thing you all can do right now is answer a few questions for me and help me figure out just what happened. Now, did any of you actually see the shooting?"

"I didn't see it happen, exactly," spoke up a small figure seated against the right wall, an older woman with crimped grey hair and a sun-bleached work dress, "but I can tell you what I did see."

"Go on, ma'am, I'm listening."

"Well, to start with I was working with my grandson in the front garden, pulling weeds. We'd been out there most of the morning, and eventually, when it was getting along towards noon, I decided I'd stop for a spell. I get short of breath so much easier these days, and my old joints just don't hold up the way they used to. . . Anyhow, I thought to myself I might step inside for just a minute and see if my Dorrie needed any help with the lunch things. I left Mattie alone in the garden. I figured he'd be fine by himself for a little bit; in a million years I never imagined a thing like this. . .

"Well, we got to talking, and what with one thing and another I suppose the time got away from me, because it was after twelve by that point, wasn't it, Dorrie? —and there was this noise out front like one of the tractor engines backfiring, not terrible loud, just sort of a popping sound. I wondered what it could have been, because far as I knew their grandfather had the tractors out in that stretch of land near Burk's Hollow, but it did make me think it was high time I went back and checked on my grandson. So out I went- and there he was, lying face down in the garden. I ran up to him and saw there was blood on his shirt and started yelling. As I was turning this way and that, crying for help loud as I could, I saw a car speeding off down the road. I didn't take much notice of it just then, but now I've had the time to think it over it seems to me a right powerful coincidence there just happened to be a car driving past at that moment."

"Can you describe the car for me?"

"I can't say I saw it any too clear, on account of the dust it was kicking up, but I can tell you it was a dark-colored sedan, maybe black or blue."

Just then Dr. Van Allen appeared at the top of the stairs, his coat slung over one arm and his shirtsleeves rolled to his elbows, wiping his hands on a damp cloth. He came down the steps lightly, his eyebrows elevated slightly above his blue eyes, and waited until he had neared the bottom before speaking.

"He's all patched up now," he said. "You can go up and see him, but go quietly, and don't tire him out with a lot of carrying on."

"How is he, Doc?" asked the boy's father.

"He's a tad shook up, which is perfectly natural under the circumstances, but apart from that he's just fine. What he needs now is rest, and plenty of it. Your son's a lucky boy, Emory. It could've been a good sight more serious, but as it is I don't think you have a thing to worry about. I've cleaned and bandaged his wounds, and those'll have to be changed each day. I'll be by in about a week to see how he's doing. He won't be able to do much work between now and then, but I can't see his having to miss more than a day or two of school. The worst that could happen to him at this point is an infection, so mind what I say about those bandages." Van Allen stepped clear of the stairwell and said in mock exasperation, "Well, go on!"

When the family had disappeared up the stairs and the three men were alone he said soberly,

"I don't suppose there's much chance, Sheriff, seeing how you dragged the major out here along with you, that this incident is as unimportant as I'd hoped?"

"Just what is it that you thought happened here today, Doctor?" Sommerlott asked softly.

Van Allen shrugged. "If it weren't for the fact of your finding a certain murdered man's body two days ago, I'd be inclined to think this was some sort of hunting accident. There are patches of woods close by here in both directions, east and west, and that hole in Mattie's back is the right size to have been made by a small-bore rifle. I have no difficulty picturing some old boy out picking off squirrels or rabbits and having one of his shots go badly astray."

Talmadge shook his head. "The bullet my deputy found is too small to've come from a rifle."

"A pistol bullet, in other words. And Perry duBree was killed with a pistol. So the two events definitely are related, then? Whoever killed Perry duBree waited four days and then decided to come gunning for Mattie Armstrong?" Van Allen glanced keenly up at the sheriff. "Why? What possible connection could there have been between Mattie and that louse duBree? Or is the man responsible for this just plain mad?"

"I won't know that 'til I've caught him, now will I?" The sheriff's mouth twitched impatiently. "Tell me about the boy's injury, Doctor."

"When I said he was lucky, I wasn't exaggerating the least bit. The bullet entered his back on the outside of his right kidney and passed through him on a slight downward angle, managing –at least as far as I could tell without cutting into him- to not hit a single vital organ along the way. Mind you, it didn't hurt that there was a lot less of him to get in the way of the bullet than there was in duBree's case.

"Of course, there's always the chance I could be mistaken about the amount of internal damage, and if he takes a turn for the worse in the next few days I'll be back out here on the double. I've cleaned both wounds, stitched and bandaged them, and I gave him a shot of codeine for the pain. Like I told them, my biggest concern right now is that the wounds stay clean and don't turn septic.

"Well, I imagine you'll be going up to talk to him now, so I'll repeat what I said before. It applies every bit as much to the two of you as it does them. Mattie needs to rest after what he's been through, not be harassed with a thousand questions he can't possibly know the answers to. You weren't planning on asking him a whole pack of questions, now, I hope?"

"Only the necessary ones," Talmadge said shortly, and headed for the stairs. The major followed.

They turned right at the top of the staircase and moved toward the sound of voices.

The drone of conversation was coming from the larger of the two boys' bedrooms. Mattie Armstrong was propped up on several pillows on a bed tucked into one corner, with his family gathered around, all apparently trying to talk at the same time. He was a pale thin boy of twelve with a cap of ruffled blond hair and a thick dressing wrapped around his shirtless midsection. His face was wan and his eyelids heavy, no doubt due to the combination of shock and codeine, but he seemed in good spirits.

Talmadge stepped into the doorway, realized that he was still wearing his hat and swept it from his head, and said, "Emory."

The boy's father turned from the bedside. Other family members lifted their heads to stare coldly at the sheriff, who was far more of an interloper here than he had been downstairs.

Sommerlott, standing behind the sheriff, found himself idly noting the features of the various relatives clustered around the wounded boy's bedside. Mattie's father was tall and brown-haired, for instance, while his son was the spitting image of his uncle, Emory's brother Burton. Burton was short and slender, with dirty-blond hair, while Mattie was tall for his age, so that the two were practically the same height; from a distance they might even have been indistinguishable.

In another family such a close resemblance might have started tongues wagging, but in this case even the most determined of gossips had been brought to silence by Burton's well-known history as a dyed-in-the-wool misogynist.

"Emory," Talmadge said as the man came near, "I need to talk to your boy about what happened. I know you want to spend time with him and make sure he's all right, but there are questions that have to be asked, and the sooner the better. And if you'll pardon my saying so, these questions'll go a lot easier if I can talk to him alone. You and your wife can stay, of course, I wouldn't think of turning you out, but as for the rest. . ."

Emory turned back to relay the message, and though the family members grumbled and muttered, with many a baleful glance at the sheriff and Major Sommerlott, they obediently filed out of the bedroom, leaving just the five of them at last. Talmadge propelled the major into the room ahead of him and closed the door behind them.

He sat down on the narrow bed beside Mattie. "Son, I reckon you know who I am. I have some questions to ask you about what happened to you today. You think carefully now on what I ask you, and tell me everything you can remember. Don't fret if it don't seem to make sense, that's all right, you just answer what you can. Now let's start with this morning, before all this happened. You were out in the garden. . ."

The boy glanced at his parents for reassurance and began to speak, softly and quickly. Sommerlott had to lean in to follow his narrative.

"Yessir. Grandma Hollis asked me to help her in the garden, pulling weeds. After a spell she got up and went inside –I s'pose she had something else to tend to- and she told me to keep working. I didn't mean no harm, I didn't really, but after a bit I got tired of sitting on the ground pulling weeds and I got up, just to stretch is all, honest. I was going to go right back to work again, I was. I started to take my hat off- it's a nice big straw hat, the one my brother Harry give me after he went up to Columbia last month and got hisself a brand-new Stetson-"

"All right, Mattie," his father said gently. "Just tell the sheriff what happened next."

"Yessir. I started to take my hat off, to wipe off my forehead, but when I raised my hand there was a noise like somebody lit off a firecracker and something hit me in the back, real hard, like the time Willie Hatch's older brother give me rabbit punches after school. I thought maybe somebody was fooling and th'owed a rock at me, but when I put my hand to my back it was awful warm and sticky, and when I looked down my hand was red all over. I started to turn 'round to see what was going on, but when I turned 'round everything sort of went blurry and tipped over- and I guess I fell down," he finished sheepishly.

"Did you see anybody or anything peculiar before you fell?"

"No, sir."

"Not even a car going by?"

"No, sir."

"Has anybody been threatening you lately? Maybe one of your schoolmates, wanting to get even with you for something?"

"No, sir."

Talmadge nodded. "Did you know the man who lived in the grey house on Ash Street, Perry duBree?"

"The big bald-headed man, the one who was new in town? Yessir, but I didn't know what his name was. He's the one got killed, isn't he?"

"That's right. You'd been to his house a few times, hadn't you?"

To the boy it was an instance of the unfathomable way adults sometimes had of knowing things that were supposed to be private and hidden. His eyes went round. "Yessir. It wasn't nothing wrong, I mean it was a secret and all, but all I did was do him a favor and carry some letters to his friends for him. He give me a nickel every time I delivered a letter, a nickel for every letter I mean, and a nickel even when there wasn't no letters. He told me to come to his house every week, to the back door so's nobody'd see me, and he'd give me the letters he wanted delivered, but I wasn't to tell a soul about it. I went to his house day before last but nobody was there and the house was all shut up. I didn't know-"

"Wait just a minute," broke in his father at last. "What's this all about? Mattie, you've been running errands for this duBree for- how long now? Sheriff-"

"Hold on, Emory, just hold on a bit, and we'll make some sense of all this," Talmadge responded. "Son, how did you first meet up with Mr. duBree?"

"He stopped me one day after school, when I was cutting home across Mr. Pritchard's back lot, and said if I wanted to make some money I could do him a favor. He had letters for his friends, personal letters he didn't want all the folks at the post office to see, and he wondered if I'd take 'em 'round for him instead. He told me where he lived, and said I was to come there every week and he'd give me the letters."

"When was this, that he first talked to you?"

"Last month, just after we had that big rainstorm."

"Who all did you take letters to?"

"There was Deacon Roberts, on South Court Street, and Mr. Carr, he lives at Mrs. Brett's boardinghouse, and Mr. Parrish, he lives above the hardware store, and- and Miss Durand who lives out on the edge of town-"

"You went to Celia Durand's house?" his mother demanded, aghast. "Matthew Thomas Armstrong-"

Talmadge continued as though she hadn't interrupted. "When you delivered these letters, did those folks give you anything in return?"

"Yessir, sometimes. Mr. duBree said I was to always wait and see if they had anything for me to take back. Sometimes they give me envelopes of their own, heavy ones, but other times they only give me a message to take back, about how Mr. duBree he'd have to wait 'til the next week. They never did say what it was he was s'posed to wait for, but Mr. duBree he knowed what they meant.

"It's funny, I reckon they must've been friends of his like he said, but they sure didn't seem real happy to be getting those letters. Sometimes they looked downright aggravated. Gosh, I wonder if maybe they're really some kind of gang, maybe bootleggers or such? And maybe the letters was secret messages, bad news for the gang?"

Talmadge smiled at the boy's youthful imagination. "You're right about those letters being bad news, at least. D'you have any idea what was in the envelopes they gave you to take back to Mr. duBree?"

"No, sir, but they was powerful thick sometimes, so I figured they was full of money or important papers, maybe."

"And those four were the only ones you took letters to? No one else?"

"No, sir."

"You're certain of that?" asked Sommerlott. "Think carefully, son. This is very important."

It was the first time the major had spoken since entering the room, and Talmadge glanced sharply at him, his eyebrows drawn together, before turning back to the boy.

"No, sir, just them."

"You ever do any other work for Mr. duBree," Talmadge asked, "besides carrying letters?"

"No, sir."

Before the sheriff could open his mouth to ask his next question the bedroom door flew open and the boy's grandfather marched in, his heavy boots scattering clods of dirt on the wooden floor. Leonard Armstrong resembled his younger son more than he did Emory, being likewise short and wiry, shorter in fact than Burton, with a full head of thick white hair. He was dressed in overalls, with a bandanna protruding from the breast pocket, and had an old faded hat in his hand; apparently he had come straight in from the fields.

"What's happened?" he demanded. "Justin tells me somebody's gone and shot Mattie. Is that right? You all right, boy?"

"Yes, Pa. . ."

"Yessir, Grandpa."

Len Armstrong glanced over his grandson briefly and swung around to shake a horny finger at the sheriff. "You! What in tarnation's this town coming to, I'd like to know. First there's this duBree, killed just this week by God knows who, and you still haven't the faintest idea who done it far as I can tell, and now this! We're not even safe on our own property now, is that it? Just what is it we pay your salary for, anyway? To sit around playing tiddlywinks while our young-uns get shot down on their own doorstep, and then go running for help 'cause you can't tell your head from a hole in the ground? Need somebody to teach you your job, do you?"

With exceptional patience Talmadge said, "If you don't mind, Armstrong, I'm trying to get to the bottom-"

The old man turned to his grandson. "Who did this, boy?"

"I don't know, sir."

"By God, I find out who's responsible for this I'll take them apart with my bare hands. Nobody comes to my home and attacks one of my grandchildren and gets away with it. . . And you, Emory, what are you doing about this? Here your own boy's been shot, and all you're doing is standing here jawing. . ."

Sommerlott watched the old man as he stood in the center of the room with his feet planted apart, swinging to berate first one person and then another, and thought that Len Armstrong reminded him of nothing so much as a banty rooster stirring up a fuss in a chickenyard. The analogy was not far from the truth: Armstrong and his wife had been forced, after a fire had gutted the house where they had lived for more than forty years, to move in under their son's roof, and these displays of belligerence were his way of reminding everyone involved that as far as he was concerned he was still the head of the family.

The old man was storming on:

"What does that fool doctor know, anyhow? It's not as if the boy has scarlet fever or some such. He'll be up and working day after tomorrow. And you," –he rounded on the sheriff once more- "what do you intend to do about this? Or do you intend to do anything? Sitting there asking a lot of blamed questions-"

"Armstrong-" Talmadge said sharply, and exhaling forcefully through his nostrils stood up. With his broad shoulders and six-foot frame he fairly towered over the other man. It was obvious in that moment that if he had wanted to he could have tossed him out of the room as easily as he might have shifted a rag doll out of his way. However, he merely said:

"You're right. I'm not accomplishing a single thing sitting here. And your grandson needs his rest."

Indeed, despite the noise and commotion in front of him young Mattie's eyelids were sagging lower and lower. Talmadge glanced at him one final time before turning to the boy's father.

"I'd appreciate it, Emory, if you and your wife'd keep what we've been discussing to yourselves for the time being. No sense spreading that sort of thing around any more than necessary. And I give you my word, soon's I have a firm idea who's responsible for all this, you'll know about it." He shook Emory's hand, and he and Major Sommerlott slipped through the knot of relatives crowded around the bedroom door and headed downstairs.

When they emerged from the farmhouse the front yard was empty save for the sheriff's truck. With the throng of onlookers dispersed to their respective homes the scene had resumed its usual bucolic aspect. On the neighboring property field hands called chaffingly to one another; in the direction of the outbuildings behind them a dog barked and fowls gabbled; somewhere not too far off a woodpecker hammered away at a tree trunk.

A single soul had remained behind. Marcus Raft was leaning against the truck's left front fender, in the process of lighting a Lucky Strike. He lifted his eyes as the two men approached and shook out the match in his hand before speaking. "Well, Sheriff? Do you have the time now to make a statement for the newspaper?"

Talmadge shook his head. "Seems to me you probably know as much by now about what happened here today as I do. You could probably tell me a thing or two. But I haven't any objection to answering a few questions on the way back into town –that is, I assume you're headed back to the square?"

Raft shook his head in turn. "Not immediately. I mean to get an interview with Mattie Armstrong and his parents, or at least somebody in the Armstrong household, before I leave here." Having made that pronouncement, the reporter appeared in no great hurry to bestir himself. "Is there anything you'd care to say about this latest attack, or about your investigation into Perry duBree's murder, that might –let us say, alleviate the concerns of the good people of Bishop's Hill?"

"I'll say this much: everything I've learned so far leads me to believe the killer's from somewhere other than Bishop's Hill, and there's been nothing about this second shooting to change my opinion."

Raft raised his eyebrows at that. "An outsider, eh? And what particularly makes you think so?"

"Now you know better than to think I'd answer that. I have to keep some cards up my sleeve."

"True enough, I s'pose. And what about you, Major? Do you agree with the sheriff's way of thinking, that the killer is from outside our community?"

"The major's opinions," Talmadge said drily, "are the opinions of a private citizen, and are his own business."

Sommerlott smiled and shrugged.

"And yet," Raft murmured, puffing sedately on his cigarette, "the town council asked him to assist you for a reason. . . Can I ask what you think's behind all this, Sheriff? The killer's motive, I mean?"

"Perry duBree had a little operation going to make money off certain people here in Bishop's Hill, and elsewhere as well, it seems like. There's no doubt in my mind that's what got him killed."

"Yes, I've been hearing about his underhanded ways the past few days. Blackmail, wasn't it? I've also heard that he was up to the very same tricks the last time he lived here, and he was forced to leave because of it. Surprising he had the nerve to show his face here again after that, but people of that sort always do seem to. Tell me –if it isn't one of those cards you're holding up your sleeve, of course- is it within the realm of possibility that he wasn't working alone, that he had a partner or partners in this crooked scheme of his? . . . Just bear with me a minute, and I'll explain the thought that crossed my mind. . . Assuming for the sake of argument that he did have a partner, and furthermore that partner is someone in the Armstrong household- what if Mattie Armstrong was shot in order to send a message to that person?"

"A warning of some kind?"

"Something like that. Why not? What else would motivate someone to want to shoot a twelve-year-old boy, and in the back at that? What could he possibly have known about Perry duBree, or about anything else for that matter, that could've made him a threat to anyone? And it would explain why the boy wasn't hurt worse than he was- whoever shot him wasn't trying to kill him, only make a point."

"It's certainly," Talmadge said, "a theory."

"But of course you won't say whether I'm on the right track or not. . . Off the record, Sheriff," Raft asked, dropping his cigarette end and grinding it under the heel of his shoe, "how close are you to actually catching the killer? The good people of Bishop's Hill aren't going to be feeling any too patient once the news of this second shooting gets around."

Talmadge snorted irritably. "It's been all of two days since duBree's body was discovered, and it takes more to solve a murder case than just snapping my fingers. I happen to think I've made good progress in the time I've had."

"I hope your fellow townsfolk see it the same way- come election time." Raft touched two fingers to the brim of his hat as he sidled between the two men and headed for the farmhouse. "Best of luck, Sheriff."

As they climbed into his truck Talmadge said, "I meant to ask Mattie if he knew of any people outside of Bishop's Hill that duBree'd written letters to, but now that I think about it I doubt he'd've told the boy any more about his little operation than he had to."

"I wonder," Sommerlott said, following his own line of thought, "if it wouldn't be a good idea to post one of your men here at the Armstrongs' in case the murderer decides to return and finish what he started. After all, it's only a matter of time before he hears that the boy's still alive."

Talmadge glanced sideways at him, and after a moment nodded. "And if Raft's right, there'll be someone here on the lookout for any suspicious goings-on?. . . I'll arrange something this evening. I don't reckon the boy's in any danger where he is.

"What's most on my mind, though," he continued, "is what Van Allen said. He made a good point. Why'd the killer wait four days to come after Mattie? I just don't have enough facts to answer that question. Could be this was the killer's first opportunity to get back here to Bishop's Hill, or could be he realized after he was home and safe again that the boy knows something that could give him away. . ." He shook his head and shifted the truck into gear.

"What do you intend to do now?"

"Now," Talmadge said, "I intend to have a good long talk with Marcel Carr, like I meant to in the first place. Something tells me if anybody can shed some light on duBree's scheming, it's him."

CHAPTER SIX

Saturday, May 16, 1931

. . .And the golden bowl gets crushed. . .

-Ecclesiastes 12:6

The man with the knife lifted his eyes in only the briefest of glances as the sheriff's truck came to a stop in front of Mrs. Brett's boardinghouse and discharged its passengers. He was sitting forward in a cane-bottomed chair on the boardinghouse porch, his wrists resting on his knees and a piece of hickory in his left hand; chips and flakes of wood slid away beneath the edge of his blade and fluttered whitely down to rest in a little pile between his feet.

A second man, lean and sallow with a pockmarked face, was resting directly on the porch on the other side of the open doorway. His response to their visitors was more affable.

" 'Lo, Sheriff," he called out. "What's the news on this shooting at the Armstrong place?"

Talmadge planted one booted foot on the boardinghouse steps. "Heard about that already, have you?"

"Yep. Clem Singer come by 'bout quarter of an hour ago and told us all about it. He didn't say who done it. You know who done it yet?"

"I have my ideas. Marcel Carr around, by any chance?"

"To be honest, ain't seen him since yesterday. You, Hi?"

The man with the knife, not even bothering to raise his head this time, replied laconically: "Not since yesterday, same as you."

Talmadge turned his head to look at Major Sommerlott. "Is that so? Mrs. Brett at home, then?"

"She's in the kitchen with Miss Millie- young Pollard's girl, that is."

Talmadge thanked the two men and he and the major stepped past them and entered the boardinghouse. It was a large building and the front hall was roomy, with a wide staircase on the left leading up to the second floor. There was a low bench along the right wall, beneath a row of pegs for hats and coats, and against the brief far wall was a short table holding a heavy, ornate lamp.

The passageway narrowed as it continued on between the kitchen and dining room toward the back of the house. As they had been told, there were two women in the kitchen, bustling from one task to another. Even with the windows and the doors open the air was hot and filled with steam. The household, it appeared, was in the midst of the transition period between luncheon and dinner, between clearing away the remains of the old meal and beginning the preparation of the new.

The older of the two women, in her forties with dark hazel eyes and long brown hair bound up in a kerchief, was the owner of the boardinghouse, Jessamine Brett. She was an attractive woman still, even with her sleeves pushed up and an apron tied around her middle, although her figure was perhaps not as slender as it once had been. She was what was commonly known as a "grass widow": after her husband had left her to run off with a car salesman's daughter from Columbia she had opened their sizable home to take in lodgers, and in the end had done quite well for herself. Her reputation as someone who kept an orderly but comfortable and cheerful house had gradually spread, and by now it was rare for her to have a vacancy for any length of time.

The second woman was less than half Mrs. Brett's age, with large china-blue eyes and a natural Dresden-doll complexion. Her honey-blond hair was easily encompassed by the kerchief around her head, for it was cut in the bobbed fashion popular among the young and smart.

When Mrs. Brett caught sight of the two men standing in the doorway, the sheriff especially, her face dimpled and one hand flew automatically, despite being covered with soapy water, to tuck in some loose strands of hair.

"Why, John! What an unexpected surprise. And Major Sommerlott too. Hello, Major. I'm glad to see the sheriff's managed to coax you out of that big old lonely house of yours –though it's a shame it has to be under these circumstances. Isn't it just shocking about the Armstrong boy? Oh, I don't know if either of you gentlemen know Miss Millicent Oakes. She's the fiancée of our young Mr. Pollard. . ."

After the introductions were complete she added, "Now don't tell me you've come to ask us questions about what's going on in this town. I'm sure I don't know what we could possibly know about it."

"Actually," Talmadge said, "I came to have a little talk with Marcel Carr, but I spoke to Hank Freley and Hiram Buckner before I came in here, and they said they haven't seen him since yesterday. Do you know anything about that?"

"You know, we were just talking about that. Seems like it's just one thing after another anymore. Mr. Carr stepped out sometime yesterday afternoon without anyone noticing and no one's seen hide nor hair of him since. I just can't understand it. He tends to keep to himself a fair bit, that's true, but it isn't like him to just go off like that without a word to anybody. I don't know what could've come over him. I've never had one of my boarders simply up and leave before, and I hope that isn't what he's done, though I know there's plenty of men, young and old, hopping trains and tramping all over the country these days. . ."

"Jess," Talmadge said abruptly, "I'm going to ask you to do me a favor. You're not going to be happy with what I'm going to ask, I know, but it'd be a great help if you'd do it. What with Marcel Carr gone as he is, and no one knowing when he'll be back, or if he'll be coming back at all, I'd be obliged if you'd slip me the key to his room. I want to step in and take a quick look through his papers, that's all. I think there's a chance he'll have something in his room that'll help me understand what all's been happening lately."

"You don't think he has something to do with these shootings?"

"I don't think he's Perry duBree's killer, if that's what you mean. But there may be something in among his papers to help point me to the man who is."

Mrs. Brett wrung her hands together. "If my other boarders see you coming in and out of his room, they'll know I gave you the key, and then where will I be? If a body can't have a private place of their own. . ." She sighed. "You're sure this will help you find out who shot Mattie Armstrong?"

"You know I wouldn't ask a thing like this if it wasn't necessary, Jess."

She turned to Sommerlott in mock appeal. "You see how he twists my little old arm, don't you, Major? And when my boarders all start packing their suitcases and leaving me because they don't trust me anymore, and I have to sell my home and go live with my maiden aunt, it'll be on your head, John. . . Oh, hang it all!"

She led them across to her bedroom, where she kept the spare keys to her lodgers' rooms. As she held one of them out to the sheriff she said archly, "I do believe this means you owe me, John."

Talmadge, who could picture with crystal keenness what his wife would say to this scene, only smiled vaguely and turned quickly on his heel.

"On the left at the top of the stairs," she called after them.

As they climbed the wide steps Talmadge said, "You follow my thinking, don't you, Major? I know Marcel Carr isn't the killer, so that leaves only one reason for him to take fright and clear out like this- he knows who the killer is, and is afraid he'll be coming after him next. What I'm hoping is he has something in his room, some clue, that'll tell me the name of this person, or at least start me on a good clear trail to him."

"It sounds plausible," Sommerlott murmured.

Talmadge reached the top of the stairs first and moved briskly to insert the key into Carr's door. Sommerlott followed a few steps behind, and when he reached him the sheriff was already turning the knob. The door opened but a few inches and then stopped, knocking against some obstruction inside. Talmadge thrust his head into the opening.

"Well," he said, his voice muffled, "he didn't go so very far, at that."

He withdrew his head and the major took his place. Marcel Carr's body was sprawled face-down on the bare wooden floor of his room, his feet against the door and the back of his head bloody. Sommerlott twisted his frame, more slender than the sheriff's, sideways and slipped through the opening and out of sight. A half-minute or so later his head came into view, shaking solemnly from side to side.

"He's dead, all right. Shall I move him to the side so that you can step in?"

"Not just yet. Come on back out here. He'll keep for a bit." The major squeezed back through the doorway and Talmadge pulled the door to and locked it again. "I'm going to call the courthouse and get Van Allen on his way over here, and then I want to talk to Jessamine Brett before I do anything else."

They marched back downstairs to the kitchen and the sheriff asked in clipped tones where their telephone was located.

"In the nook under the stairs," Mrs. Brett said. When Talmadge had disappeared around the corner she asked, "Did you- did you find what you were looking for, Major?"

"Not exactly," Sommerlott said quietly.

Mrs. Brett flashed him a quizzical look and went back to her washing-up. A few moments later the sheriff reappeared in the kitchen doorway.

"Jess," he said, "can you stop what you're doing, please? I need to talk to you."

She turned and saw the expression on his face. "Yes, John," she said immediately, wiping her hands on her apron. "Millie, would you mind. . .?"

"Yes, of course, Mrs. Brett. I'll just finish up these potatoes, and. . ."

The two men followed Mrs. Brett along the passageway toward the front of the house and through the doorway at the foot of the stairs, into a smallish room filled with furniture. Apart from several lesser pieces, the parlor held a firmly-upholstered sofa and matching armchairs, a player piano, a desk and straight-backed chair, and a short bookcase, all decorated with a pleasant feminine hand.

She perched uncertainly on the edge of the sofa. "What is it, John? What did you find?"

"Let me ask the questions I have first, Jess, and then I'll explain about Marcel Carr. When exactly did you see him last?"

After a brief reflection she said, "I s'pose it was yesterday at lunch. At least, that's the last time I can recall. In the afternoons, if he hasn't anything pressing to do, he usually retires to his room to read the newspapers and study his racing sheets – gambling, that's his weakness, though Lord knows we all have our own- and I imagine I just naturally assumed that's what he did. If I talked to him at all after lunch was over I don't recollect it, and honestly with a household to run I'm far too busy to spend much time visiting with my boarders until the evening. I think the first any of us realized we hadn't seen him was at suppertime. We eat at six o'clock, you see, but I always call them down a few minutes 'til so they can wash up and have a last cigarette before they eat –I don't allow smoking at the dinner table, it's just a little rule of mine- and when the table was all set and I stepped to the back door to call them inside I saw they were all there except Mr. Carr. None of them knew where he'd gotten to. Now I know things are bound to come up unexpectedly from time to time, but to simply go off without saying a word to a soul- but his disappearance does have something to do with these shootings, doesn't it? You've found something in his room that tells you that?"

"You're sure none of your other boarders had any ideas about his going missing?"

"No, it was a complete puzzle to us all. I waited for a few minutes just in case he'd been delayed for some reason, but he never appeared, and so I decided to go up to his room to see if he wasn't feeling poorly- I half figured he might've taken sick or something, and was laying down and resting.

"And do you know, of all the coincidences, who should I see when I come into the hall but Mr. Frank Hitchens, headed up to the second floor and looking for Mr. Carr the same as I was! I declare, I was a bit surprised by his coming in like that, without so much as a how-do-you-do to me. 'Course I realize my boarders are going to have visitors occasionally, that's only natural, but after all this is still my house, and Mr. Hitchens is usually such a gentleman, everyone says so. . .

"At any rate, I said to him, 'Why, Mr. Hitchens,' I said, 'how you startled me. I didn't hear you come in. Is there something I can do for you?'

"Of course he come back down the stairs then and told me all about it, how he was looking for Mr. Carr, and how they had some personal business to take care of and Mr. Carr'd made an appointment with him for six o'clock. Well, I said that was right strange, since six o'clock was our supper hour and

Mr. Carr knew that well enough, he's been living here for nine years. Then I told him about no one knowing where Mr. Carr'd gotten to, and in the end we went up to Mr. Carr's room together. I knocked on his door but there wasn't any answer, and I even went so far as to try the doorknob, but the door was locked, and so I knew he must've gone out without our noticing. If he'd been sick in bed there'd've been no reason for him to've locked the door."

"What did Mr. Hitchens say to that?"

"He didn't say much of anything, just sort of shook his head and apologized for startling me and went on his way. Now, John, what's this all about? What did you find up in Mr. Carr's room?"

"Hold on, Jess, I'm not through with my questions yet. Do you know if Carr kept a pistol in his room?"

"Good heavens, I don't think so. John. . ."

"Mrs. Brett," asked Major Sommerlott, "did Mr. Carr own an automobile?"

"No, I don't believe he ever has owned one. As far as I know when he has to go out of town any distance he takes a ride with one of his friends, or with someone else who has a car. Not that he goes out of town very much at all. And of course when he has an appointment here in Bishop's Hill he simply walks, the way most of the rest of us do."

"Do you know if any of his friends drive a blue automobile?" he continued.

"I surely don't. . . John, I can't stand this suspense any longer. What on earth is going on?"

Talmadge took a deep breath, but before he could launch into an explanation Deputy Christie appeared in the parlor doorway, with Dr. Van Allen behind him. This time, Sommerlott noticed, the doctor had not bothered to bring his black medical bag with him.

"Where is he, Sheriff?" asked Christie.

"Upstairs," Talmadge said tersely. "Door directly to your left at the top of the stairs. It's locked, but I'll be there with the key shortly." He turned to a wide-eyed Mrs. Brett. "I'm sorry, Jess, but there's no easy way to say this. Marcel Carr's dead."

"Oh my God," she said in an exhalation, and jerked unsteadily to her feet. "And he's up there-"

Talmadge had risen at the same time, and caught her by the shoulders as she took a tentative step toward the door. "No, Jess. There's no point in your going up there. Major, why don't you fetch Millie Oakes in here to sit with Mrs. Brett until we're done?"

The woman sank back down onto the sofa, dazed. "And he's been up there dead this whole time? We've been marching around this house merrily as you please, and all the while-" She collapsed limply into one corner of the sofa, her hands pressed to her mouth and her face ashen.

When the sheriff and Major Sommerlott finally joined the doctor and Deputy Christie outside the victim's room, the hallway and the stairwell leading up to it had begun to fill with people, his fellow boarders and others. Such is the rapidity with which news moves in a small town, especially news that has traveled along a telephone wire past the eager ears of a quidnunc of an operator. Talmadge unlocked Carr's door and used his shoulder to push it open enough for the four of them to enter, and then turned and closed it firmly in the faces of the onlookers.

Van Allen knelt next to the body and ran silently through his examination, at one point taking a wooden depressor from his vest pocket and probing gingerly at the back of the victim's head, while the others tried their best in that small space to give him room. With the four of them and the body the bedroom was practically filled to capacity.

At length he stood and addressed the sheriff. "Seems straightforward enough. Someone stove in the back of his head with a heavy object, probably straight-edged. Otherwise there are no injuries anywhere on him as far as I can see, excepting a good-sized mark where his forehead hit the floor on the way down. Looks like your killer decided to change his style."

"Something like this, then," interposed Major Sommerlott, indicating a square Art Deco clock sitting atop the victim's bureau, all bronze and sharp edges, with dark reddish-brown stains across its upper back.

"That would've done the trick, all right. No sign of *rigor mortis* yet. Generally speaking, it takes about twenty-four hours for a body to go good and stiff –less than that if the temperature's sufficiently high. Considering the time of year and the fact that that window's closed, I'd say around two o'clock yesterday afternoon is a safe bet for an outside limit on when he was killed."

"That narrows it down a bit," Talmadge said, "but not near as much as I'd like. Thank you, Doctor. Empty his pockets, Nate, and then run down to the doctor's car and fetch up his stretcher. We'll use one of the sheets from the bed to cover him up when you take him downstairs. I don't imagine Mrs. Brett will mind that a single bit."

While they waited for the deputy to return the sheriff and Major Sommerlott poked through the contents of the victim's pockets, and then proceeded to search the room for anything that might conceivably have been a clue, while Van Allen took his turn at attempting to stay out of the way. It was not a lengthy search. Apart from the narrow bed and the bureau in the near corner upon which stood a washbasin, the bloody clock, and a chipped mirror, the room held only an abbreviated writing table and accompanying chair. Racing forms and tip sheets were strewn across the table, while newspapers and cheap magazines were piled carelessly on the floor beside it. A number of photographs, some framed and some simply tacked to the wall, hung above the table. It was quickly apparent that there were no incriminating papers or letters secreted anywhere in the room, no revolvers tucked away out of sight.

"Doctor," Talmadge asked toward the end of the search, "have you been rinsing your hands in this washbasin?"

"I have not."

"Hm. This water's bloody. If it wasn't your doing —and I can see Carr wasn't in the middle of shaving himself when he was killed- then that means the killer stopped and washed his hands 'fore he left this room. I wonder why he took the time?"

"No doubt for the same reason he changed his *modus operandi* in this case. We are, after all, standing in the center of a building full of people."

Talmadge lifted his head. Major Sommerlott had spoken from the other side of the room, where he was scrutinizing one of the photographs mounted above the writing table. It was a framed picture, an enlargement of a section of a group portrait, and showed men in drab uniforms gathered in ranks in a sun-browned field. Though the faces of the men had been blurred somewhat by the enlarging process, across the margin at the bottom of the photograph someone had printed plainly: *9th Regiment, Camp Jackson, S.C., August 1917.*

Talmadge, conscious of a sharpness in the other's voice and recalling the questions he had asked Mrs. Brett, said wonderingly, "You were thinking Marcel Carr might be the killer, weren't you?"

Deputy Christie entered with the stretcher tucked under his arm, banging the poles against every available surface in his attempts to maneuver in that small space. When he had it unfurled the sheriff and Van Allen rolled the body carefully onto it, and Talmadge pulled a sheet from the bed to cover the corpse. During all of this the major, his hands clasped behind his back, did not once remove his gaze from the wall above the writing table.

"Clearly," he muttered, "I was mistaken. . . This must be Marcel Carr with the X above his head. Just before they shipped out, I assume. And this looks like Burton Armstrong, and unless I miss the mark this fellow is Perry duBree. . ."

The sheriff, who was close enough by then to see what he was looking at, replied off-handedly, "Like you said yourself, Major, nine-tenths of the young men in this county fought with the same regiment."

He stepped around his deputy to the doorway, gesturing to one of the more strapping onlookers, and when the man came near enlisted him to help carry the body down to his truck. There was some consultation while the man and Christie worked out who would take which end of the stretcher, and then with a count of three they were on their way, with the doctor following after and making an occasional pointed comment about their handling of the corpse.

"Do you mind if I take this photograph with me?" Sommerlott asked.

"Suit yourself, Major. Makes no difference to me. Though I imagine Carr's folks'll want it returned eventually."

Sommerlott slipped the photograph from its nail and started to move toward the sheriff, but then stopped abruptly and pointed at the floor. "There's something there, just where Carr's feet were lying. Is that-?"

Talmadge had caught sight of the object at almost the same moment, and bent to scoop it up. It was a key. He dug the key he had used to enter the room from his pocket and held the two up side by side to the light, then turned and tried the second key in the door.

"It's the key to this room, all right. In fact, it's pretty well identical to the one Mrs. Brett gave me. Now what the devil does that mean? If Carr had his key with him all along, how'd the killer come to lock the door behind him? He certainly couldn't've fixed it from the inside, and then walked out through a locked door. . . Just how many keys are there to this room, I wonder? Or did Carr manage to lock the door before he died? Why would he do that? And if he had,

wouldn't he've been facing the other way?"
Talmadge shook his head in irritation.

"I don't think the explanation is as mysterious as you're making it," Sommerlott said patiently. "Take a moment to look at the door, and you'll see what the answer is."

Talmadge grasped the door by its edge and swung it on its hinges, frowning as he looked it over. Apparently no solution presented itself, for he shook his head again and released it. He took a long last look around the room to determine whether he was leaving anything undone, and then he locked the door and he and Major Sommerlott headed downstairs.

All the way down to the parlor the two men were peppered by the spectators with questions and comments ranging from encouragement to jeers, but the sheriff marched stolidly on as though he heard none of it, and the major followed mildly in his wake. Mrs. Brett was still resting on the parlor sofa, though she was sitting upright once more, with Millicent Oakes beside her holding her hands. The room was fairly teeming with people, some hovering solicitously nearby and others traipsing in and out. Talmadge returned both keys to the woman, sent Miss Oakes out to round up Mrs. Brett's five remaining boarders, and then proceeded to empty the room of bystanders.

When all of the boarders had been assembled and the closed door barred the parlor to everyone else, the sheriff led them through the questions he had previously put to Mrs. Brett. The results, after almost an hour's worth of diligent review, were nil. Like their landlady, none of them could recall having seen Marcel Carr at any point after Dr. Van Allen's time limit of two o'clock the previous afternoon, nor did they remember any visitors to the boardinghouse before Frank Hitchens' arrival around six p.m. Talmadge sighed and thanked them and they went out in a group, discussing the murder with zest. Mrs. Brett declared that she had to get back to her kitchen, killing or no killing, and she and Millie Oakes departed, leaving the sheriff and Major Sommerlott alone in the little room.

At length Talmadge said, "Seems to me I might could be mistaken about this second killing. I was thinking Marcel Carr was just another of Perry duBree's victims, who happened to figure out the killer's identity and had to be put out of the way. But what if he was actually in on this blackmailing scheme, a partner with duBree? In that case it could be he was killed out of revenge, and not just 'cause he knew who the killer was."

"I wonder," Sommerlott said.

"Yes, this all does tend to upset your theory on the crimes, doesn't it, Major? . . . I think I'll come back here again tomorrow and run through all this a second time with these folks, go back even further this time, take them through the last month or so and see if they can shed any light on Carr's activities. There might be a clue of some sort there somewhere." The sheriff sighed again and stood up. "Right now, though, I'd best be headed over to Carr's parents', to hopefully break the news to them before some wag-tongued busybody does it first. I doubt you'll want to come with me for that. After that unpleasant task is done I intend to go home, eat my wife's fine cooking, put my feet up, and not talk to anybody else the rest of the evening.

"I'm afraid you'll have to walk over to the courthouse to be driven back to Shiloah, 'less you want to use Mrs. Brett's 'phone to call for your car to be sent 'round. Deputy Christie'll've gone with the truck by now."

"That's quite all right. I was considering stopping at the courthouse anyway."

Talmadge glanced down at the other man out of the corners of his eyes. "I know I asked you this once already today, Major, and believe me I'm not trying to be impertinent, but you sure you don't have any ideas about these killings you're holding back from me?"

Sommerlott shook his head gloomily. "No, no ideas. All I have at the moment are questions."

Talmadge gave a brief, surprising bark of laughter. "Well, at least that makes two of us."

He held open the parlor door and the two men shook hands in the doorway. Sommerlott tucked the photograph he had taken from Carr's room under his arm and made his way past the people still milling about- in the corridors of the boardinghouse, on its porch, in its yard. Despite the numerous stares of curiosity cast in his direction no one called to him or dared question him. By the time he reached the sidewalk the sheriff had emerged onto the porch and had both hands raised in the air, attempting without much success to quiet the demands and imprecations being thrown at him. Sommerlott caught sight of Marcus Raft standing at the edge of the crowd; the reporter, instead of joining his voice with the rest, had his head turned and was watching the major walk away with a thoughtful expression.

Although it was the drowsy part of the afternoon, that long lazy time leading up to the dinner hour, there were plenty of souls about in the streets. The news of Marcel Carr's murder was spreading rapidly and, coming as it did almost simultaneously with the announcement of the attack upon young Mattie Armstrong, was having a galvanic effect on the town. It was no longer a matter of an unpopular and abrasive heel being killed in some out-of-the-way manner; now, with this latest assault, with the victim having been struck down in his own home, it had become impingent. People talking on porch steps and at garden gates turned their faces toward the major as he passed, their conversations dropping sharply in volume and in some cases ceasing entirely. Tensions and uncertainties were on the rise, spurring suspicion and distrust, and unless an answer were found soon the sheriff would have on his hands a community near the breaking point.

When he reached the courthouse Sommerlott found only one person in the police station, Deputy Anders. In many ways Olin Anders was a contrast to his fellow deputy: under medium height and stocky, with fair hair and pale, protruding eyes, he was slow of thought and reaction but thorough and conscientious at whatever tasks he was assigned. He looked up at his visitor with a friendly smile.

"Hello, Major. 'Fraid the sheriff's not in right now-"

"Yes, I'm aware of that." Sommerlott dragged a chair up to the deputy's desk and laid the photograph in front of him. "As a matter of fact, I was just with him. I came here with the hope that there might be someone in the courthouse who could tell me a little something about the men in that picture. Do you recognize any of them yourself? This one is Marcel Carr, of course, and I believe that's Perry duBree. . ."

"This have something to do with the killings?"

"I don't know. If we could identify each of the men in that photograph it might be a start to answering that question."

Anders picked up the photograph with both hands, pressing his eyebrows together in concentration. "This one here looks like Emory Armstrong's brother, and this one's Dalby Sutter. . . Major, I reckon I know somebody might could help us with this. Amos Peck, the night watchman at the bank. He fought in the Spanish War when he was younger, and he had a boy killed in Europe in the last war, in some place called Shadow Terry-"

"Chateau-Thierry," Sommerlott murmured.

"-And so he's been interested in wars and such most all his life. Sort of a local historian, you might say. Why don't I send somebody to fetch him 'round for us? He don't start his watch at the bank 'til sundown, and he'll be plumb glad to sit down and chew the rag 'til then. If you don't mind, Major, I'll just 'phone over to Anson's and have 'em send across some sandwiches for us all. . ."

A little less than a half hour later the three of them were gathered around a tray bearing ham-and-cheese sandwiches, bottles of cola, and coffee, deep in conversation. Amos Peck was in his early sixties, with white hair and steel-blue eyes, short and powerfully-built, and proved to be a veritable gold mine of information regarding local participation in various military campaigns. After squinting and holding the photograph in question up to best catch the light he began to rattle off a steady stream of facts, naming each young man in the picture and giving a brief biography as well. Sommerlott picked up pen and paper as the man spoke, and by the time

Peck was finished he had a list of eight names in front of him, two of them with check marks beside them. Peck, knowing he had done well, reached to pour himself another cup of coffee and then sat back with a self-satisfied expression and launched into a reminiscence of his experiences at Las Guasimas under General Wheeler. Sommerlott drew the deputy's telephone extension to him and asked the operator to connect him with Cole Grayson.

After a moment or two Miss Bernetta Mayhew said, "I'm sorry, Major, there's no answer at his home. Would you like me to try his sister's for you? He spends a fair amount of his time there."

"Yes, thank you."

Shortly thereafter Grayson's good-humored voice came over the line, with a tinny babble of voices in the background. "It would have to be when I have a winning hand for the first time this afternoon that I get called to the 'phone. Hello, Major. What can I do for you?"

"Are you working on anything for Mr. Davenport at present?"

Cole Grayson held a rather unusual position in Bishop's Hill. Although he filled most of his time by doing odd jobs here and there around the town, his real talents emerged in his employment by the township lawyer, Bernard Davenport, on those few occasions when that worthy had some matter that required investigation. Somehow, despite most everyone in the community knowing that he worked for Davenport, Grayson always managed, whether through charm or cleverness or some combination of the two, to ferret out the exact facts being sought.

"No, sir, not just now. . ."

"Good. Do you have a pen and paper handy? I have some names for you to take down."

"Fire away."

Sommerlott read off the six names on his list without check marks. "Those men all served in the same squad during the War. I'd like to know where each of them is now. Also, I'd like to know whether Penny Jewkes has mentioned to anyone any visitors to Perry duBree's home apart from the ones she named to the sheriff and myself."

"Mm-hm. These men have something to do with what's going on in our town, I take it?"

"If I knew that, Mr. Grayson," Sommerlott said drily, "I wouldn't need your help, now would I?"

Grayson chuckled. "No, I expect not. I'll get back to you soon's I can, Major."

CHAPTER SEVEN

Sunday, May 17, 1931

". . .And you must return to me with the evidence, and I will go with you; and it must occur that, if he is in the land, I will also search for him carefully among all the thousands of Judah."

-1 Samuel 23:23

Major Sommerlott settled into one of the chairs on his verandah, looking out over the stretch of lawn sloping down to the road, and dropped his folded coat and hat across his lap and thought that it was rather a shame. To have to be called upon to leave the peaceful seclusion of his estate, where just then the only sound to be heard was the restful whispering of insects among the foliage. . .

On the other hand, it meant a way of occupying his time. He had earlier returned from church and eaten the cold lunch that Hecate Sowers had set out for him, and then, with no personal business to attend to and nothing to do in aid of the sheriff's investigation until Cole Grayson reported back to him, he had been faced with the usual question of how to while away the empty hours of a Sunday afternoon. He had taken down at random a dusty volume from his library shelves and had retired to the study.

The study of the great house was in a sense the major's eyrie, the room in which he felt most at ease. Due to his grandfather's unique sense of architecture, the section of the house containing the study was elevated by several steps above the rest of the first floor rooms, making of it a sort of high corner tower from which he could look out over his land and fields, much as a sea captain might gaze out upon the wild and restless infinity of his demesne. Too, that corner of the building, facing the southeast as it did, received the most sunlight, and so it was the one room whose curtains and windows were generally kept open.

He had thus relaxed in a comfortable armchair, with his legs stretched out on an ottoman and the volume he had selected, the *Cometographia* of Increase Mather, open upon his lap- and with predictable results. Before too long his head had begun to nod forward and his eyelids droop.

When the metallic burr of the telephone broke in upon his drowsing, causing his eyes to fly open, he had for a brief moment no idea what the sound was. When the realization came to him he thrust a slip of paper into the tome in his hands and spun toward the doorway, calling out, "I'll get that, Mordecai!"

It had not, however, been Cole Grayson on the other end of the wire.

"Sheriff Talmadge, Major. I'm going to have a little talk with Celia Durand now, and I s'posed you'd want to be along to hear what she has to say. I'll be out there to your place in fifteen or twenty minutes- unless, of course, you're otherwise occupied?"

He raised his eyes now as the sheriff's truck made its slow, rhythmic progress up the long lane leading to the house, and recognized that under the circumstances the other man's haste was perfectly understandable. The community held him responsible to put an end to whatever it was that was going on in their town, especially now that the killer's attacks numbered three, and without a doubt Talmadge was feeling the pressure of that responsibility.

When at last the truck had pulled into the curve of the driveway and Sommerlott was installed in the cab, Talmadge tapped his breast pocket significantly.

"I finally have those two lists I was after –got them late last night- and I'm on the right track now. I'll see exactly where I stand after I've talked to Celia Durand. . .

"I'd've called for you sooner, but I got into conversation with young Joe Orton, Hughie Orton's boy, coming out of church this morning. He was telling me how surprised he was by this latest killing, since he reckoned he'd seen Marcel Carr just before it happened. I asked him what he meant by that, and he said he was in the drugstore with some friends Friday afternoon when Carr come in to buy a packet of tooth powder, a few minutes before four o'clock he figured. You see how that narrows down the time frame I'm dealing with. With Carr being seen alive at the drugstore at four, and Frank Hitchens and Jess Brett finding the door to his room locked at six. . .

"The question I'd really like an answer to is how the killer managed to slip into Carr's boardinghouse during that time without a soul seeing him."

"Did any of Carr's fellow boarders observe him stepping out to the drugstore that afternoon?" Sommerlott asked socratically.

"If they did, they haven't said so to me." Talmadge glanced sidelong at his passenger. "You haven't come to some conclusion I should know about, have you, Major?"

Sommerlott shook his head. "I have no more ideas today than I had yesterday. I did set Cole Grayson to uncover some information for me, but I have yet to receive any word from him."

Talmadge grunted noncommittally, and they travelled on in silence.

A short time later the sheriff's truck came to a stop in front of a small house on a road leading southward out of the town. It was a tidy Victorian cottage, dark brown with modest bargeboards and vermilion trim, with a scattering of woods around it and along the opposite side of the road. Clusters of various flowers grew in the space in front of the house, and on the porch twin rocking chairs were separated by a narrow square table. Directly in front of the door was parked a small red roadster with its top folded down.

According to the gossips of Bishop's Hill, the color of the car was highly appropriate- for Celia Durand was the "scarlet woman" of the community, a young lady of questionable morals and dubious income, who dressed in too worldly a fashion and who smoked and drank and swore as often and as well as any man. Here in the semi-isolation of her little cottage, with the nearest neighbor several hundred yards away and screened from sight by the trees, she freely entertained her various beaux, of whom there were of course a number, though probably not nearly as many as rumor granted her.

When she opened the door in response to the sheriff's knock Sommerlott saw that she was around twenty-five or so, with medium-brown eyes and smartly-bobbed hair a shade or two darker. Her ruby lipstick was applied in the "bee-sting" style that Hollywood had lately made popular. With her heart-shaped face and slim figure she was not unattractive, but her prettiness was marred somewhat by the hard lines of her expression, a hardness not fully erased by the ironically welcoming smile she wore. Though it was the middle of the afternoon, she was clothed in a flowered negligee with a rose-and-violet housecoat over it.

"Why, hello, Sheriff. Let me see if I can guess the reason for this visit. . . Actually, I've been expecting a visit from you ever since I heard that Perry duBree's worthless carcass had been uncovered. And your friend is-?"

"Major Sommerlott," said he, tipping his hat.

"A pleasure to meet you, Major. I've heard of you, of course, like everyone else in Bishop's Hill. I just didn't know that today would be the day we'd be introduced. Well, won't you gentlemen come in?"

The heels of her mules clacked on the wooden floor as she led them inside. The little house was expensively furnished, with some elegant pieces that had probably come from the showrooms of the large department stores in Columbia or Atlanta. The parlor, which was through the first doorway to the right, held a low yellow sofa and a black walnut coffee table, a pair of high-backed armchairs and some others without arms, a cream-colored telephone on a square table, and vivid throw rugs scattered here and there. A tall phonograph stood with its cover off and its arm poised in mid-air. She had apparently been in the midst of opening packages when they arrived at her door, for empty boxes and wrapping paper were piled on the coffee table and one end of the sofa, while other, unopened boxes were stacked on a chair next to the telephone table.

She sank down onto the sofa and reached for a narrow silver box with turquoise inlay that rested on the coffee table. Taking a long, thin cigarette from it, she leaned forward and held it expectantly to her lips. Talmadge dragged a packet of matches from his pocket, struck one, and bent over her. She drew deeply on the lit cigarette and leaned back, crossing her legs languidly and smoothing the skirts of her dressing gown over her knees while regarding him from under lowered eyelids.

"Now, Sheriff, just what can little old me tell you?"

"First of all, you might tell me just where you were yesterday around noon."

Celia opened her eyes wide in surprise. "Yesterday? I thought you were here to ask me about-"

"Don't worry, I'll come 'round to him soon enough. Now, as I was saying. . ."

"Yesterday," she repeated. "As a matter of fact, I was up at the county seat almost all of the day with my good friend Lillie Painter, from Lawrenceville. We were doing a little shopping, as you can see." She waved a hand airily at the pile of boxes. "Why ever on earth do you ask?"

"You haven't heard what's happened?"

"Our little town doesn't put out its newspaper on Sunday, as you well know- and my neighbors don't exactly come running to me with the latest news. So no, I have no idea what you're talking about."

"I see. What time did you leave Bishop's Hill yesterday?"

"Around ten o'clock in the morning or thereabouts. Something of an early start to the day for me, to be honest. I generally prefer to sleep in a bit more. . . I drove up and met Lillie at her parents' home, and we went straight on to the county seat from there. I didn't get back here until almost sunset."

"You drove the car parked out front?"

Celia smiled indulgently. "It's the only one I own, Sheriff."

"Of course it is. What I meant was, the two of you rode up to the county seat in your car, and not your friend's?"

"Lillie lives with her parents, and doesn't have a car of her own."

"Right. Now you didn't happen to make any other stops while you were in Lawrenceville, did you? Say at the home of Jubal Inglethorpe- he's your cousin, isn't he?"

Celia Durand's eyes were cold and flat as chips of sandstone. "I did not. That branch of my family is one I have as little to do with as I can, and, you may be surprised to hear, they generally feel the same way about me."

"So you're saying you didn't visit him at all yesterday?"

Celia sighed and turned her face away. "No, Sheriff, I didn't."

"Care to tell me when you spoke to him last?"

"I really cannot recall."

"All right. Do you happen to own a pistol?"

She swung her gaze back to the sheriff and said wryly, "Now you've finally gotten 'round to a question I can see the point of." She rose and crossed with a half-unconscious swaying of her hips to the telephone table. Opening its single, shallow drawer, she drew out a small black automatic and held it out to the two men with both hands, its squarish barrel flat against her palm. It was an unassuming weapon but dangerous enough, in the major's estimation a .22 or something in that range, the sort of pistol with which a woman might feel comfortable.

"A young woman in my position, living all alone," she said disingenuously, "needs a little protection. . ."

"D'you have any other guns in the house?"

"Mercy, isn't one enough? I'm not Annie Oakley."

"Let's go back a day," Talmadge said when she had put the pistol away and resumed her seat on the sofa. "Where were you on Friday afternoon, between four and six o'clock?"

"So now it's Friday, is it? Are you intending to go through every day of my week. . .? Well, hard as it may be to believe, I was here all day Friday, doing my washing up and other housework. I do occasionally feel the urge to do something of that sort."

"There wouldn't happen to be anyone who could testify to that?"

Celia laughed scornfully. "Hardly! I'm not usually in the habit of gathering an audience to watch me rinse my stockings."

"Tell me about Tuesday morning. Around nine o'clock. Were you up and about then?"

"Now," she said with a canny expression, "we're getting to Perry duBree's long-overdue demise, aren't we? These are the questions I've been waiting for. No, if I was at all awake then, I hadn't risen yet. I believe I lingered in bed for another hour or two that day before I even got up and made breakfast."

"And of course there's no one to verify your alibi for Tuesday morning either?"

"Actually, I had a gentleman with me then. He arrived Monday evening and stayed until Tuesday afternoon. His wife happened to be away with her sick mother for the week, and the poor dear was feeling lonely. I trust," she said after a brief pause, "that you aren't going to be tiresome and ask me for his name?"

"What sort of car does he drive?"

"He has a big black Packard, very stylish." Celia leaned forward for another of her narrow cigarettes and lit it expertly from the remnant of the first. "I'll ask you again, Sheriff- you don't intend to try talking me into naming my visitor, do you? After all, he's no one you know- at least, I can't imagine he is- and a lady likes to think that her friends are entitled to some degree of privacy."

"Unfortunately, not everybody feels the same way, isn't that so? Perry duBree, for instance. When did he first start blackmailing you?"

Celia took a long pull on her cigarette, her face wooden, before replying. "About a month ago, just after he'd moved back here. He hid in the woods across the road there with one of those cameras of his and snapped pictures of some of my gentleman friends as they came in and out of my door. He threatened to send the photographs on to their families unless I gave him what he wanted. Now some of them I don't suppose would've minded if he'd had their pictures printed in every newspaper from here to Beaufort, but all the same I decided it was best to go along with his schemes, at least for the time being. I happen to value my home in my little corner of our community."

"And so he sent Mattie Armstrong around with letters demanding money."

"That was later. At first he suggested we might work out a different. . . arrangement." Her eyes were far away as she spoke, and one hand unconsciously caressed the ribs beneath her left breast. "After one night of that I'd taken as much of it as I ever meant to. I slipped away to the parlor here as soon as I was sure he was asleep, and when he woke up he had the barrel of that little gun of mine against the side of his head. I told him to get his clothes on and get out, and if he ever tried to set foot in my house again I'd put a bullet between his eyes. He tried to grab the gun out of my hand but I kept out of his reach, tried to threaten me, reminded me of the photographs he'd taken, and I told him plainly that it didn't make a speck of difference, he wasn't ever going to have the privilege of putting his hands on me again. I asked him if he wanted me to pull the trigger and show him just how serious I was.

"In the end he instead suggested that, in addition to paying him certain sums of money every so often, I'd pass on to him any bits of scandal and gossip that happened to come to my ears. I agreed to do it mostly to get him out the door, but don't think for a moment I feel the least bit guilty about helping him. The way the good God-fearing people of our fair town treat me, it seemed only right to drag a few of their sins and errors out into the light."

If the two men were at all shocked by Celia Durand's frankness, they gave no sign of it. The sheriff asked merely,

"How often did Mattie bring you letters?"

"Once a week, generally, toward the end of the week."

"When was the last one?"

"Two weeks ago, I believe. Actually, if somebody hadn't finally decided to put Perry duBree down like the worthless cur he was, I expect I'd've been getting another letter from him any day now."

"I don't s'pose," Talmadge drawled, "that you have any notion who that somebody might be?"

"Of course not, Sheriff. No idea at all. I will say this, though- far as I'm concerned, whoever it was deserves a parade and a medal."

"Hm. I think that's all the questions I have for you just now, then- unless the major has some questions of his own?"

It had not been meant as a serious invitation, but Sommerlott surprised the sheriff by responding. "Just one, actually. Did you ever pay a visit to Perry duBree's home, Miss Durand?"

"Never. He never suggested it, and there's no way I'd ever agreed if he had."

"Then I don't suppose you'd know of anyone who did visit him at his home, perhaps more than once? Ah, well. Thank you anyway."

As they climbed into the sheriff's truck Talmadge said, "You see how she was trying to be clever, showing us that little pop-gun of hers so innocently, when it's far too small to've been the gun that killed duBree? And I reckon the fact that she only has an alibi for the first attack and the last, but not for the afternoon Marcel Carr was killed, is significant, too."

Seeing his passenger's blank expression, he added: "Don't worry, Major, I'll explain what I mean soon enough. Right now, though, I'm going to call on Perry duBree's other two victims and get an accounting of their movements, even if they don't have a single thing to do with these killings. I wouldn't want the town council to think I wasn't being thorough, after all."

From the secluded lane where Celia Durand had her home they drove north, past the square, to one of the better neighborhoods of Bishop's Hill, a street lined with large houses with well-maintained lawns and manicured hedges. The house they stopped in front of was of pale tan with dark shutters and strands of wisteria spiraling up the porch pillars, and belonged to one of the deacons of the Methodist Church.

The front door was opened to Talmadge's twist of the bell-pull by the maid and cook, a cherub-faced, wide-hipped black woman who looked long and hard at them through the screen and then went away bellowing: "Sheriff to see you, Mist' Roberts. . ."

She returned shortly and ushered them into the study, which was smaller than the major's at Shiloah and somewhat oppressive. It was a typically masculine room, all dark woods and leather, with Civil War mementoes and hunting paraphernalia adorning the walls.

Guy Roberts stood up from behind his desk and shook his visitors' hands. He was a broad-shouldered, firmly-fleshed man with good-humored but canny black eyes. The black hair on his round head, though receding at the corners, was waved and oiled, and his suit, if not the newest, was at least of a distinguished cut. He waved them to firm but comfortable armchairs.

"Welcome, Sheriff, Major- er, take the gentlemen's hats, Alberta. You'll excuse this clutter, I'm sure- I was just going over the congregation's accounts for the final time. Can I offer you anything in the way of refreshments? We have no spirits in the house, of course, but then man does not live by wine alone. . . No? All right, that'll be all, Alberta.

"Now," he said, folding his hands together, "what can I do for you, Sheriff? I trust this visit has some connection to the attacks occurring in our town?"

Talmadge nodded. "I won't take up much of your time this afternoon, Deacon. I just have a couple of questions to ask you, purely as a matter of routine you understand, in regards to Perry duBree's death. To speak plainly, I know about duBree's blackmail letters, and how Mattie Armstrong brought them 'round to your house for him. Now, can you tell me where you were yesterday around noon?"

The various lines of Roberts' face tightened subtly and his mouth twitched. "So you know all about it, do you? And you somehow imagine that I went forth in the heat of anger and struck down that poor foolish boy because of the part he unwittingly played in duBree's schemes? Sheriff, I am surprised at you. After all the years we've known each other I should think you'd know better than to imagine I'd be involved in anything so underhanded and cowardly."

Talmadge replied to the blandest of tones. "As I say, Deacon, these are just routine questions. Doesn't really matter what I think, I have to ask them, else certain folks'll be asking why it is I didn't."

Roberts sighed and glanced aside. "I s'pose you're right. People do tend to want to think the worst, don't they? Very well. Yesterday I had a brief luncheon here at home and then I stepped 'round to visit Charlie Shales, over in Pershing Street. Charlie has been a good friend of mine for several years. I believe it was about twenty after twelve or so when I went, though I didn't actually look at my watch at the time, and I was there for at least a couple of hours."

"Seems clear enough," Talmadge said. "Can you also tell me where you were Friday afternoon between four and six o'clock?"

"Friday afternoon? I spent the better part of Friday, from two o'clock onward, with Gilbert Wallings and Bert Horval at the courthouse. Young Gil is the mayor's assistant, as you well know, and we've been working on some preliminary arrangements for the upcoming Independence Day celebration. Personally, I think the festivities are just what our community needs. Times are hard right now, there's no denying that, and the Good Lord only knows if it'll get worse before it gets better, but even so there's plenty of reasons for us all to be proud to be living here in this great land, not like those godless heathens over there in Russia and Africa. I hope we'll be able to put together enough of a jamboree to remind the folks of Bishop's Hill of everything we have to be thankful for. And it's less'n a month and a half away now- time for us to get the ball rolling. . . I trust these killings'll be long behind us by then, Sheriff?"

"I'm sure they will. Now you say you were with Mr. Wallings and Mr. Horval the entire afternoon?"

"Well, most of the afternoon, at any rate. We had my wife's oldest brother and his family over here to dinner Friday evening, and so I had to cut the discussion short in order to be in time to meet them when they arrived."

"What time did you get home?"

"A few minutes before six."

"Fine. Now what about Tuesday morning, around nine o'clock? Can you recollect what you were doing then?"

"Tuesday morning I was with Harley Copes in his office at the hardware store. You know, of course, that aside from keeping the congregation's books, I lend my services to the shop owners of our fair town on occasion, to help them in keeping their ledgers balanced- for only a modest fee, that is. Christian charity would hardly permit me to charge them more than that."

Guy Roberts had worked as a clerk at a large factory for several years in his youth, and was the closest thing to a bookkeeper that the township had. In a rural community where most people had only a basic education, and a good number were entirely illiterate, his services were enough in demand that his exercise of "Christian charity" had gleaned him a tidy profit.

"I was there from around eight o'clock, before the shop was open, to ten o'clock or shortly after. If Harley Copes' word on that isn't enough, you can ask his two assistants. They came in and spoke to me when they arrived to open up for the day, a few minutes before nine."

"Much obliged, Deacon," Talmadge said easily. "Do you keep a pistol in the house, by any chance?"

"I have my father's pistol, yes. A Colt revolver- which I keep right here in my desk drawer, as a matter of fact. If you feel you need to see it. . ."

The sheriff waved his hand. "Quite all right. Don't trouble yourself. Truth is, that was the last question I had for you- although I do believe the major has one he'd like to ask. . ."

Sommerlott glanced briefly at Talmadge and repeated the question he'd asked Celia Durand- with the same result.

"Visit Perry duBree's home? Not on your life, Major! There wasn't one single thing in this whole world that would've induced me to spend a minute more around that no-account leech than I had to."

The sheriff thanked Roberts for sparing the time to talk with them and the two men started to rise, but their host, with a quick look at the closed door, began speaking before they could.

"Sheriff, you've known me for many a year now. I wouldn't want you –or you either, Major- to go away with the wrong impression, thinking that Perry duBree's demands for money meant more than they did, that I was somehow floundering in iniquity. I stumbled, I freely admit that, I gave in to a moment of weakness, with that girl here in front of me, but I'm sure when you've heard the whole story-"

"To be perfectly honest," Talmadge said, "I'd rather not know. 'Afternoon, Deacon."

When they were sitting in his truck once more he said, "I s'pose you're wondering why I didn't ask him quite as many questions as I did Celia Durand? Believe me, Major, I know what I'm doing."

He paused for a moment with his hand resting on the gear lever, the truck droning underneath them, and went on meditatively: "I have to say, I think this attack on Mattie Armstrong's the last one we'll see. I don't believe the killer will be coming after anyone else. First he killed Perry duBree, who was blackmailing him, then Marcel Carr, who was either in on the blackmail scheme or knew something incriminating about the killer (you see I haven't made up my mind on that yet), and then finally he went after the boy who'd been delivering the blackmail letters. That last one seems to me to've been more spite than anything else, though it could be he was trying to get rid of a potential witness as well. 'Course all that's only a rough outline, but at any rate, I can't see there's anybody left for him to strike out at now."

Sommerlott said simply, "I hope you're right."

"But you won't be convinced 'til you've heard what Cole Grayson has to tell you? Well, you haven't heard the evidence I've uncovered yet."

They headed back toward the center of town, but just before they came into sight of the courthouse Talmadge turned to the right, into the alley that ran behind the shops that lined the north side of the square. Their destination this time was the residence of Oliver Parrish, who worked as a salesclerk in the general store and lived in a pair of rooms over the hardware store. Talmadge climbed out and marched unhesitatingly up the long flight of flimsy-looking wooden stairs that led to Parrish's apartment, the major following cautiously behind. He hammered on the door once and a second time, but there was no answer.

"Looking for young Parrish, are you, Sheriff? I'd think you'd have better luck in the morning."

The two men descended to the alley. The speaker was Carter Lacey, who with his wife owned and operated the town's one clothing store, which of course had separate entrances for male and female customers and a discreet partition running down the middle. He was in his shirtsleeves, leaning on the bottom half of the Dutch door at the rear of his shop and puffing complacently on his pipe.

"He isn't home, then?" asked Talmadge.

" 'Fraid not. He's gone up to Lawrenceville for the day, to visit with his aunt and her family. Won't be back until late this evening, probably."

"Sounds like you have a fair idea of his comings and goings."

"We are neighbors, after all." The Laceys similarly lived in a set of rooms above their shop, although their kitchen was located on the ground floor, just beyond the Dutch door and around the corner. The smell of frying meat wafted out to them even as they stood there. "Though I wouldn't claim to know all he gets up to, driving here and there in that jalopy of his, with that lot of young Apaches he keeps company with –and every one of them toting a hip flask, too. You can't hide a thing like that from an old tailor like me. There's just no telling what trouble a pack of hellions like that are capable of stirring up."

"So you'd know pretty quickly if he wasn't where he usually is," Talmadge said, as much to himself as to Lacey. "Say for instance this past Tuesday, around nine a.m. You'd know if he wasn't opening up the general store as usual?"

"I would, and so would the junior clerk, Billy Chappell. Far as I know, though, he was at work Tuesday morning same as always."

"And the same thing'd be true about Friday afternoon, between four and six o'clock? He'd've been at work then?"

"Well, they'd've closed up shop at five, like we all do, and then spent the next hour or so cleaning up and getting things ready for Monday, so. . ."

"I don't imagine you'd know where he was yesterday around noon?"

"Can't say as I would." Lacey squinted speculatively at the sheriff. "This all have something to do with these killings we've been having? They've got my wife and her friends fair rattled, I have to tell you."

"I'm just sorting out loose ends, that's all. I'm sure, as an old tailor, you know how that is. Thank you, Mr. Lacey."

As they came around the corner into the square Talmadge said, "I wanted to question all three of Perry duBree's victims, in case there was a chance of picking up any little bits of useful information, but the truth is it's Celia Durand who's the important-"

He broke off as they came to a stop in front of the courthouse. Deputy Anders had emerged and was standing at the top of the steps, calling clamorously to Talmadge and waving his arm back and forth energetically. As soon as they reached the base of the steps Anders burst into speech.

"Telephone call for you, Sheriff. It's Cole Grayson. He's out at the Hawley place, and something's happened. I've been waiting for you to get back. . ."

Talmadge took the courthouse steps two at a time and strode through into his office, the other two close behind, leaving the door wide open as he went. He snatched up the earpiece of the telephone.

"Sheriff Talmadge here. . . Hello? Cole?. . . Where? What were you doing there?. . . He's *what*?. . . All right. I'll want to hear every word of this. I'll get hold of Dr. Van Allen, and the major and I'll be there shortly. You meet us there. And be sure you tell the Hawleys and whoever else is listening in on this line to stay clear of the place. I don't want a crowd of gawkers in my way."

Talmadge slapped the earpiece onto its hook and glared at the figure standing in his doorway.

"What the hell," he said distinctly, "is going on in this town, Major?"

CHAPTER EIGHT

Sunday, May 17, 1931

For it is the day of confusion and of downtreading
and of confounding. . .

-Isaiah 22:5

Talmadge pressed his foot down on the
accelerator and the truck groaned up the curving dirt
path from the road to the top of the dusty hillock.
Major Sommerlott sat on the far side of the cab, with

Deputy Anders sandwiched between them. Van Allen's black Model T, with the doctor and Deputy Christie in it, came following after.

Cole Grayson was waiting for them on the porch of the cottage that squatted on the little hill, and when they came into view he gestured toward the side of the house, where a brown truck spotted with rust was parked, and his low roadster behind it. He dropped down over the edge of the porch as Talmadge brought his truck to a halt and swung down to the ground, but the sheriff moved past him without a word. The smell struck them while they were still a dozen or more steps away, and Sommerlott pulled his handkerchief from his pocket and clamped it over his nose and mouth.

"Good and ripe, isn't he?" murmured Van Allen from behind him. "Excuse me, Major. . ."

There was little enough for the doctor to do when he reached the truck except confirm what their senses were already telling them. The body of a man in his early forties, clad in dingy overalls, sat behind the wheel, his bearded head lolling to one side and his dark green eyes staring emptily forward. He had evidently been in the act of climbing into or out of the cab when the killer approached, for the driver's-side door was hanging open. There was a dark, scorched hole in his left temple, just behind and above his left eye, and blood had spattered the inside of the windshield and the seat alongside him. From where he stood Sommerlott could not see what was left of the man's other temple, and he had no desire to. The inside of the truck was thick with flies, jittering across every available surface.

"I'd say there's no doubt about what killed him, eh, Doctor?"

"None that I can see. A single gunshot to the head at point-blank range, which it appears he wasn't expecting- but then really, who of us does expect it, even now? By the state he's in I'd estimate he's been dead longer than Perry duBree was when he was found- say three or four days, this time."

"Mm. Nate, you and Olin get him out of there, then empty his pockets and scout around the truck, inside and outside, for anything that might be evidence. Doctor, I'm going to leave them in your hands for the time being. The rest of us. . ."

Sommerlott had stepped forward when the body was removed and was peering into the cab. "There shouldn't be any trouble in finding the bullet, Sheriff. There's a scratch in the opposite doorframe, a place where the metal is gleaming through, where it must have struck and ricocheted-"

"Don't worry, Major, my deputies'll find it. Right now, though, if you don't mind, the three of us are going to go inside and have a little talk. There are some questions I'd like to hear the answers to."

The dead man, Hall Anglin, had been a life-long bachelor, and his property, especially the cottage, had the sort of appearance one would expect under the hands of an unmarried man living alone in the country. It was a mere shack more than anything else, on which he had done just enough work to ensure that the roof didn't leak too badly and the windows weren't too drafty in the winter. It was divided into two rooms, the first of which appeared to be little more than a storeroom. The second room was the one in which he had actually dwelt, with a narrow bed covered with tatty quilts squeezed into the corner nearest the pot-bellied stove, and the cabinets, icebox, and single table all buried beneath a layer of unwashed dishes, empty cans, foodstuffs, and other clutter. The sheriff shoved as much of it aside as he could and the three of them sat down around the little table.

"I want to get one thing straight right off, Major," he said bluntly. "Were you expecting this? Cole said something over the 'phone about your sending him out here to find Anglin."

Sommerlott shook his head. "I had no expectations one way or another. A certain vague possibility had occurred to me, which this latest discovery tends to confirm, but I'd be interested in knowing what else Mr. Grayson has found out. . ."

The two of them turned to look at him. Cole Grayson was a husky young man with curly blond hair and bright grey-blue eyes, with a perpetual cheeriness and good-naturedness about him, an air of being at ease in all sorts of company- a quality which no doubt served him well in his investigative forays for the township lawyer, Davenport. Even now he sat at the end of the table with a relaxed and untroubled expression, turning his cloth cap over in his hands.

He described the charge he had received from the major the previous day, the list of six men he was to locate, and Talmadge held up his hand.

"What six men would this be, Major? And what the devil do they have to do with Perry duBree and his victims?"

Sommerlott began to explain about the military photograph that had been hanging in Marcel Carr's room, and the sheriff nodded briefly and turned back to Grayson. "Go on."

"The first man on the major's list I had no trouble finding. I saw Frank Hitchens at church this morning with his son, and when I was talking to him afterwards he said he was planning on spending the rest of the day relaxing at home- the way folks tend to do on a Sunday afternoon.

"The next man on the list was Paul Turner. I drove out to Hobb's End to his house, but there was no sign of anybody 'round the place, and his neighbors told me they hadn't seen him since Wednesday evening. They have a juke joint fixed up out that way in an old farmhouse, not too far from the county line, with dice and cards and a jazz band and all the rest of it- you know the one I mean, Sheriff?"

Talmadge nodded, as briefly as before. "I know about it."

"Well, that was the last place anybody remembers seeing him. Seems he and his pals have a poker game there every Wednesday and Sunday, regular as clockwork, with a table set up just for them in one of the back rooms. This Wednesday evening, about eleven-thirty or so, maybe closer to midnight, he ran out of cigarettes and decided to go get some more. Now they have cigarette girls out front there in the main room, but he said he had a fresh pack in his car. The rest of 'em didn't think anything of it – they'd just finished one hand and were about to start another, and he'd left his chips there on the table- they figured he simply felt the need to stretch his legs. Eventually, when he didn't come back, a couple of them decided to go looking for him, and found that his car was gone. The management hadn't paid any attention, people come and go there all hours of the night, but the fact is no one's heard from him since."

"What color is his automobile?" asked Sommerlott.

"Sorry, Major, didn't know I was s'posed to find that out."

Talmadge only repeated: "Go on, Cole."

"From Hobb's End I headed over here. Hall Anglin was the next man on the major's list, of course. It didn't take me any time at all to find his body when I got here. I looked around the place a bit, but there was nobody around that I could see and no telephone, so I had to drive down the road 'til I found a family that had one, and finally fetched up at the Hawley farm."

"That leaves three more men for you to track down, I take it?"

"Possibly only two," Sommerlott said. "One of the names on the list I gave Mr. Grayson was Burton Armstrong's."

"Yes, you won't have to worry about anybody coming after him- that is what's in the back of your mind, I s'pose? I deputized Eb Olsen last night, last thing before I went home, since he lives just down the road from the Armstrongs, and he's sitting on their front step right now with a shotgun across his lap. Anybody tries to come near the place that doesn't belong there, whoever they're coming after, and they'll be staring down the length of his double-barreled."

Talmadge reached into his inner breast pocket and took out two pages folded together. "Now that I've heard what you've had Cole working at, I do believe it's time you heard the facts I've uncovered. I think you'll see they hang together pretty well.

"You recall my saying I'd finally gotten those lists I was waiting for? Well, here they are. The blue automobiles registered in this part of the county and their owners, and the names of Perry duBree's lodge brothers. And wouldn't you know, there's a name shows up on both lists.

"But before I get to that, I want to go over the points against the three suspects so far, that is, Perry duBree's three remaining victims. Now you know I never figured the killer come from Bishop's Hill in the first place, but all the same let's take a look at what we've been told about the three of them, and see what kind of picture it gives.

"First of all, Guy Roberts. Deacon Roberts said he was with Harley Copes in Copes' office from eight to ten o'clock Tuesday morning, and if that's true there's no way he could've been meeting duBree in front of his house at nine. He told us he left a meeting in Gil Wallings' office at the courthouse on Friday afternoon in time to be home a little before six, so it's possible he could've stopped in at Mrs. Brett's boardinghouse during the time in question and did away with Marcel Carr. It wouldn't've been the least bit out of his way. As far as where he was yesterday, he claims to've gotten to Charlie Shales' place about twenty minutes past twelve, which means he'd've just had time to drive past the Armstrong farm and fire a pistol at young Mattie. So, two possibilities out of three. On the other hand, his name isn't on either one of the lists I'm holding.

"Now Oliver Parrish. On Tuesday morning he'd've been behind the counter of the general store, and Friday afternoon he'd've been cleaning up the shop with the other clerk and setting the stock in order for Monday. If he hadn't been in the store as usual either one of those days someone would've been bound to notice, and with all that's been going on lately I'd've heard tell of it by this point. As for yesterday, he could well have an alibi for that attack, too. I don't know. I do know that his name isn't on these lists, either.

"And finally, Celia Durand. She claims to have been entertaining a visitor until Tuesday afternoon, which, should she decide to tell me his name, would give her a clear alibi for the time Perry duBree was shot. As for Friday afternoon, it's just the opposite. She says she was home alone all day doing her laundry and other housework, without a single soul to verify her story. And she s'posedly spent the whole day yesterday up at the county seat with a friend of hers, so she couldn't possibly have been anywhere around when Mattie Armstrong was shot.

"You probably wondered, Major, why I even bothered questioning her, when we all know the killer's a man. There's a good reason, believe me. You recall my asking her about a cousin of hers who lives in Lawrenceville? Well, whose name do you s'pose showed up on both the lists I asked for? That's right. Celia Durand's cousin Jubal Inglethorpe, known to his friends and family as Jube, owns a blue 1926 Oakland sedan and belongs to the same K. of P. lodge Perry duBree was a member of.

"That'd be some coincidence, if it was a coincidence. No, the way I figure it's like this: Last time Perry duBree lived in Bishop's Hill Celia Durand would've been a child, so it's not likely he knew the kind of young woman she is beforehand, before he moved back here. I'd say he probably heard about her from the fellows at his lodge –maybe even from Jube Inglethorpe himself- and struck on her when he was scouting around for targets for his blackmail scheme. And who else would know the secrets of this little town like she would? So Celia Durand ended up becoming his first victim in Bishop's Hill this time around, and then through her Oliver Parrish, Guy Roberts, and Marcel Carr.

"But eventually she had enough of his squeezing her for money, and worked up a plan to get rid of him. She roped her cousin into her schemes and had him use his car and pistol to kill duBree. They're members of the same lodge- who better to take the victim off guard and get close enough to him to do him in? And she figured nobody here'd ever make the connection between the two men- Inglethorpe doesn't live in Bishop's Hill, after all, and there's probably not too many folks here who'd know him by sight. A girl like that, I don't reckon she had the least trouble wrapping her cousin 'round her little finger and getting him to do just as she pleased.

"You see how she arranged the whole business? She had her cousin lure Perry duBree out into the countryside and kill him on Tuesday morning, and made good and sure she had an alibi for when it happened. Then when it was time to do away with her next victim, Marcel Carr that is, and it would've been too difficult for Inglethorpe to approach him, she undertook to do it herself. Remember that she hasn't any way of proving where she was Friday afternoon. She probably beguiled one of the other men boarding at Mrs. Brett's into slipping her inside, and now that he knows what he made himself a part of he's afraid to speak up. Then, the next day, after providing herself a solid alibi once more, she sent Cousin Jube after Mattie Armstrong.

"If Inglethorpe hadn't given himself away by dropping his lodge pin when he snuck into duBree's house Tuesday night to take away the blackmail photos and what all, her scheme might've worked, too.

"When it comes down to it, it may be Celia Durand never originally meant to go after Mattie Armstrong. After all, it's clear enough the boy doesn't really know the first thing about what Perry duBree was up to. But think to yourself when he was shot- on Saturday morning, after you and I'd been out to Wash-town the previous day and heard Penny Jewkes tell how he'd been coming 'round to duBree's house to deliver those letters. By the time the news of our visit, and what we'd been told, got back to Celia Durand's ears –she's never been too choosy about who she takes to her bed, and I imagine after a certain point those young bucks'd tell her anything she wanted to know- she put two and two together, realized the Armstrong boy could throw suspicion in her direction, and decided he had to be put out of the way before he could talk. Fortunately for all of us her cousin isn't much of a marksman, and I got to hear the evidence she was trying to cover up."

"In his defense," Sommerlott murmured abstractedly, "it isn't easy to hit a target, even a stationary one, from a moving vehicle."

"I'll take your word for that, Major. You'd know better than I would. At any rate, it explains how the killer had the nerve to drive right up to his victims' houses in broad daylight, in his own car. Apart from Celia Durand, there may not be anybody in this town who'd know Jube Inglethorpe's car when they saw it, even if they happened to get a good look at it.

"Well, by now you're probably wondering how I'm going to fit this latest killing, and Paul Turner's disappearance, into the picture I've put together. And I have an answer for you. What if Perry duBree wasn't alone in working his blackmail schemes, but had others in it with him? Mattie Armstrong fancied he was delivering letters for some kind of gang, and it could just be he wasn't far wrong. I expect Hall Anglin was killed because he was a part of the blackmail ring right alongside duBree.

"And it could be Paul Turner was as well, and realized they'd be coming after him next, and so he skipped out of the county to save his neck." The sheriff shrugged. "Or it could be he'd finally run up his gambling debts past any chance of him being able to pay them back, and he decided to take a powder for that reason. I don't know enough yet to know which of those possibilities is more likely.

"It could even be Celia Durand wasn't duBree's only means of finding new victims. Paul Turner's a regular at that roadhouse out past Hobb's End, and Marcel Carr with his racing forms, and Oliver Parrish and his flask-toting pals, might well've ended up there in due course. . . And what if duBree's little crime circle was involved with more than just blackmail? That roadhouse isn't the only place of its kind in this end of the county by a long shot, and with the quantities of liquor they have to be going through in a week's time, there's liable to be any number of folks who have a hand in moving the stuff."

"I've heard it said Anglin kept a good-sized still in the woods behind this house," put in Cole Grayson.

"That could well be." Talmadge sighed aggrievedly. "I've been asked more than a few times why I don't do something about the roadhouses and gin mills out along the county line. Truth is, I don't have the funds or the manpower to go chasing 'shine runners back and forth across the county. It's the federal government who decided alcohol had to go, and if they want those laws enforced they're going to have to provide the men to do it. It just isn't in my power to keep a lid on it."

He shook his head. "All that's beside the point. Can you see, Major, that all I've said so far makes sense, more sense than thinking these killings have something to do with Marcel Carr's old Army squad? The War ended thirteen years ago. Why would somebody wait until now to start killing off soldiers?

"Of course, I admit a good part of the case against Celia Durand and Jube Inglethorpe is just speculation until I get some solid facts about him. Who knows, I could be wrong about some of the details. I'm going to get hold of the town deputy in Lawrenceville, Cy Burrows, tomorrow and see what he can tell me. Hopefully between the two of us we can manage to pin Inglethorpe's hide to the wall. Meantime I'll have to talk to Anglin's neighbors up and down the road here, and see if any of them noticed anything suspicious in the last few days, any strangers in the area. I doubt you'll want to follow along on my heels while I do that, Major."

Talmadge pushed his chair away from the cluttered table and stood. "Well. Time to go see what my deputies have found."

Sommerlott turned to Cole Grayson and said, "About the two men on the list I gave you who have yet to be accounted for. . ."

"It'll take a bit more doing to track down those last two," Grayson replied, still kneading his cap. "I heard Judd Scott moved to Lawrenceville a few years back, and Fred Sears moved up to the county seat just after he returned from Europe. It could take a little time to find out where they are now. If it's all the same to you, sir, I'd rather wait until the morning before driving up that way."

"Before you do that," Talmadge said, "I want you to drop into my office first and give me your official statement on how you come to find Hall Anglin's body."

He stopped in the doorway with his hand on the knob. Sommerlott was standing with one hand on the back of his chair and the other balled into a fist on his hip, and was looking around himself with a frown.

"Something on your mind, Major?"

"I was considering," Sommerlott admitted, "asking Mr. Grayson to assist me in searching this cabin, on the chance that there might be something here which could have a bearing on these killings, but it strikes me that it would be practically impossible to find anything of import in this rat's nest."

"Probably so. But you're right, it's one of those jobs that'll have to be done. I'll assign one of my deputies to tackle it in the morning. Right now, though. . ."

They followed him outside. The deputies had laid the varied but mundane contents of Hall Anglin's pockets out on a cloth beside the sheet-wrapped body in the back of the sheriff's truck, awaiting his perusal, and were standing nearby. Nate Christie was apparently in the middle of relating some long and self-serving anecdote to the other deputy, while Dr. Van Allen leaned against his car a little ways off and regarded him coolly.

While Talmadge poked stiffly at Anglin's belongings with his forefinger Christie said, "We found the bullet that killed him, Sheriff. It'd bounced around the inside of the cab, like the major figured, and was under the passenger-side seat."

"Right. Keep good hold of it. The two of you can take the doctor with you when you drive the body and all into town to the undertaker's –afraid I'm going to have to borrow your car for the rest of the evening, Doctor- and if you want to ride with them as well, Major, one of my deputies'll have no problem sitting in the back next to the late Mr. Anglin. Or I'm sure Cole-"

"You're going to have to what?" Van Allen interjected, his expression a mixture of affront and disbelief. There followed a brief but vivid discussion between the two of them, with the doctor giving vent to several trenchant comments, but in the end he sighed and climbed into the sheriff's truck between the two deputies.

As the sheriff bent to wind the crank of the Model T Major Sommerlott slid into Cole Grayson's low-slung roadster and said, "If you don't mind, instead of taking me directly back to Shiloah, let's drive into town and pay a visit to Frank Hitchens."

"Sure thing, Major," Grayson said, settling his cap jauntily on his head. "You don't really think he'd know anything that could help the sheriff, though?"

"There is a slim possibility that he may have some salient fact or facts in his possession without even being aware of it. And at this point we cannot afford to leave any avenue unexplored. There's most assuredly a pattern of some sort to these deaths, but what that pattern is I do not yet know. I need more information."

With that pronouncement he closed his mouth firmly, and the rest of their ride passed in silence.

The Hitchens home was a large structure in the Second Empire style, of pale grey stone with blue-grey shutters and trim, located of course in one of the better neighborhoods north of the square. Well-manicured grass covered the high ground on which it stood, and a tall, stately hedge ringed the property. Flowering vines overspread a trellis along one side of the porch.

The household included Hitchens and his son and three servants. Hitchens' second child, a daughter, had died shortly after her birth eight years earlier, and his auburn-haired wife had followed a week later.

The major left Grayson parked by the gate and mounted the steps to the wide porch, where the bell was answered, not immediately, by the manservant, a stocky, smooth-skinned black in his early- to mid-forties.

"Is Mr. Hitchens at home?"

"Is he expecting you, suh? The family is about to sit down to supper. . ."

"He isn't. You may let him know, however, that I wouldn't think of calling upon him like this unless it were important, and that it relates to the sheriff's investigation. You recall who I am? –Major Sommerlott."

"Of course, suh."

A few minutes later the servant returned and ushered the major into the parlor of the house, a room appointed in grey and scarlet. Shortly afterward Frank Hitchens came in, dressed in a dinner jacket. He was stocky and square-jawed, with bright black eyes, a long nose over a thin mouth, and thick black hair. At his temples strands of grey were creeping through, an unexpected sight in a man of forty-four. He smiled pleasantly and somewhat curiously.

"No, no, don't get up, Major. It's a pleasure to see you again, even if I wasn't prepared for it. I'm afraid we're just sitting down to dinner. . . I expect you've sent the boy who drove you around to the back? My cook, Cora, will have ginger snaps or some such for him."

"Actually, I was driven by Cole Grayson this time."

"And he's waiting outside?" Hitchens turned immediately to a small table and rang the little bell sitting upon it. When the manservant appeared he said, "Vernon, step out to the car sitting in front of the house and ask Mr. Grayson in. Give him a glass of tea or anything he'd prefer."

It was not until that was done, and Cole Grayson was installed in the parlor alongside them and nursing a glass of iced tea, that Hitchens drew up a chair for himself and sat down across from Sommerlott.

"When Vernon first told us that you were here, Major, I thought perhaps you had some further questions about the arrangements we'd worked out this past week for your sharecroppers. But he said that you were calling on behalf of the sheriff?"

"In a manner of speaking. As far as my 'croppers are concerned, I'm quite satisfied with the terms you were able to set out for them. . . and while I'm on that subject, let me say that I appreciate very much your making the time to discuss the matter with me. Your son was telling me beforehand how busy you've been lately."

Hitchens smiled and leaned forward conspiratorially. "Major, can I let you in on a little secret? I haven't even told Henry yet; in fact, I intend to break the news to him at the dinner table this evening. I plan on running for county commissioner in the next election, and I've been crisscrossing the county from one end to the other meeting with various committees and what have you, attempting to get things in order for my campaign. You might be amazed at just how much work such an undertaking involves."

"No doubt. Congratulations."

"Now, don't congratulate me until I've actually won the election- or at least until I've made my first campaign speech! So, how can I help you this afternoon?"

"Something has arisen in connection with the attacks here in Bishop's Hill, and I thought perhaps you'd be able to provide some information for me, even to suggest a potential line of inquiry."

Hitchens straightened up in his chair, with a faint frown creating lines between his eyebrows. "Certainly I'll be only too glad to answer any questions you put to me, Major, but I hardly think I'm likely to point to anything the sheriff hasn't already thought of. Personally, I'm finding it all rather hard to take in. This madness- here, in our quiet little town. What is it now- three victims in four days?"

"Four, actually. A little over an hour ago Mr. Grayson here discovered a man named Hall Anglin shot to death outside his home on Armellis Road."

Hitchens murmured something and passed his hand over his forehead.

"Yes. Now if I may, I'd like to ask you about your visit to Marcel Carr on Friday afternoon- or rather, your intended visit. Mrs. Brett mentioned that you called there around six o'clock. Would you tell me about that?"

"I don't know that there's much to tell, unfortunately. Mr. Carr asked me to come to his room at six because that's the usual dinner hour at Mrs. Brett's, and we'd have some privacy in which to talk. There was some business we had to discuss- well, I don't s'pose it matters now what it was. I was on my way up to his room when Mrs. Brett came into the front hall and saw me there, and quite naturally inquired as to what it was I wanted. I came back down the stairs and explained why I was there, and we went up together. There was no answer when she knocked on his door, of course, and when she tried the knob she discovered the door to be locked. At the time I assumed he'd had to step out unexpectedly, without being able to leave a message for me, and I took my leave. If I'd had any inkling he was lying dead on the other side of that door. . ."

"Did you happen to notice anyone in the vicinity of Mrs. Brett's boardinghouse when you arrived?"

"You mean that I might've seen the killer fleeing the scene of his crime? No, I don't really recall anyone in particular. There were people out and about on the street, of course, but they were just regular folks. . ."

"And you noticed nothing that struck you as peculiar or unusual, either at the time or later?"

"I can't say that I did, no."

"This business between the two of you- I assume it was purely financial in nature? You had no other reason for paying Mr. Carr a visit?"

Hitchens stared blankly at the other man. "What other reason did you have in mind, Major?"

"I'll come back to that in a moment," Sommerlott said. "Now as to Perry duBree- I believe you visited his home on occasion as well?"

"Once or twice, yes. And he came here once. He had some money-making scheme he wanted me to invest in. it was questionable to say the least, and when I'd learned all the details I refused to have any part in it."

"I'm going to ask the same question regarding him as I did about Mr. Carr. Do you remember seeing anyone coming or going when you visited him, anyone who sticks out in your mind- perhaps someone you saw later at Mrs. Brett's boardinghouse?"

"Afraid I don't." Hitchens shook his head. "This is a small town, Major. I'm bound to see plenty of the same faces over and over, day in and day out."

"Of course. Have you had any unexpected callers recently -other than Mr. Grayson and myself, that is- strangers or persons you hadn't seen in some time, perhaps calling while you were out?"

"Neither my son nor Vernon have mentioned any unusual callers, and I haven't had any that I can recall. Just what are you getting at, Major?"

"Allow me to ask another question in an effort to answer yours. How closely do you keep in touch with the men with whom you served in the War- in particular, the men of your squad?"

"I- I don't follow you, Major."

"Let me speak plainly. Within the past week three men who served in your Army squad have been killed, another has disappeared, and a fifth may have had an attempt made on his life. Can you think of anything, any reason at all, that could have provided someone with the impetus to come after those men?"

Hitchens shook his head again, looking slightly dazed. "Apart from those men living here in Bishop's Hill who I see on a regular basis, I haven't really kept in touch with the members of my old Army squad. Truthfully, Major, I try not to think about those days any more than I have to. We had a trying task to undertake, and we did what we had to do, but I don't spend my time reminiscing about it. A man has to live in the present, not hide himself away in the past, and I have quite enough to keep me occupied without revisiting those days."

"Then you haven't spoken with any of the surviving members of your squad recently? You wouldn't have any idea of their current whereabouts?"

Hitchens rose to his feet and began to pace. "You really think that's what's behind these killings? As I say, I don't generally make a habit of reminiscing about those days. . ." His voice changed slightly from its usual brisk, matter-of-fact tone, became slower, more thoughtful. "I don't have to tell you, Major, how it was then- the parades, the speeches, the flag-waving. We boys were young and keen and proud to be called up for our country, and our families and the rest of the community were proud for us, in our nice stiff new uniforms. We were so certain that we were just going to march over there and show the Kaiser and his Huns who they'd picked a fight with, learn them a lesson they wouldn't soon forget. We found out quick enough it wasn't going to be that simple, it wasn't going to be Teddy Roosevelt and the Rough Riders charging gloriously up San Juan Hill. You recall the conditions we were faced with as clear as I do. The taste of the trenches in everything we ate, the muddy water up to our ankles whenever it rained, ice cold in the winter and stinking and verminous in the summer, the shelling, the feeling when those big guns fired like being shaken by the hand of God Himself. . . and in the end, all that fighting and dying for a few square miles of dirt. What did it all really accomplish? Nothing worth talking about, far as I can see. . .

"I'll ask you again, you're certain these killings have something to do with the War?"

"It strikes me as a possibility."

"It's just too far-fetched. The War ended thirteen years ago. . . Major," he said quietly, turning to face him directly, "I know you had some hard experiences over there, harder even than the rest of us maybe, and what with living in that old house of yours all alone, shut away behind drawn curtains, it could be you've had too much time to brood on old troubles. Perhaps those days are weighing more on your mind than they ought. . ."

He trailed off, seeing Sommerlott's unnaturally empty expression, and said quickly:

"No. You stagger me. I'm sorry, Major, I can't conceive of any such thing. Couldn't the connection between these deaths be something much simpler? . . . Since the sheriff didn't accompany you here this evening, should I take it that he has a different point of view of all this? Perhaps to do with Perry duBree's blackmailing activities? I've been hearing some of the rumors going 'round about that. Isn't it far more likely that that's the root of it?"

"Everyone seems to agree that it's the most sensible answer," Sommerlott said drily, as he rose to his feet in turn. "Thank you for your time, Mr. Hitchens."

CHAPTER NINE

Monday, May 18, 1931

Will not those devising mischief go wandering about?

-Proverbs 14:22

They came around a slight curve and rattled over the wooden bridge across the Satchee, smaller and trickling here, and as the woods to the right of the road fell away the bright blue water tower of the town of Lawrenceville came into sight. Major Sommerlott had the thought that he always had when he passed this way: that Lawrenceville seemed larger, more prosperous, more genteel than Bishop's Hill. It was an illusion, of course, since the two towns were of more or less the same size and standard of living, and arose mostly from the arrangement of the streets. Whereas Bishop's Hill was roughly squarish in shape, Lawrenceville was distinctly rectangular, being only a few blocks across, and its north-south streets had been fashioned into long, quiet, tree-lined promenades.

They motored along past individual farms and simple cottages which grew ever closer together and became rows of comfortable houses with tidy lawns and neat picket fences. A little farther on there were shops and small warehouses, and just the other side of these was downtown Lawrenceville. On the right was the town hall, with the jailhouse behind and beside it, and a tiny post office. In back of those buildings stretched the green expanse of the town park, on the far edge of which was the knoll bearing the splay-legged water tower. To their left were the bank and the Knights of Pythias lodge hall, the movie theater, and the drugstore, all bracketed by various storefronts. Out of sight somewhere in that same direction was a matchbox-sized railway platform, built to meet the L&N railroad where it came curving in from the southwest; beyond the tracks was the black section of town.

For the trip into Lawrenceville the sheriff had borrowed his brother-in-law's car, and he pulled it into the alley that ran alongside the town hall to the jailhouse. They climbed out and went inside the little stone building, where the sole deputy was sitting behind his desk opposite three empty cells.

He jumped to his feet when he saw them and held out his hand. Cy Burrows was a lanky young man with an unruly shock of chestnut hair and an open, genial expression on his rawboned face.

"Hello, Sheriff. Just got back to my office 'bout half an hour before you 'phoned. Good timing, hey? Fact is, I been a good sight busier'n usual the last couple of days. And this gentleman is-?"

"Major Sommerlott. He's assisting with my investigation."

"Glad to meet you, Major. Now, Sheriff, you said you wanted to have a talk with Jube Inglethorpe?"

"That's right. I'm hoping something'll come up in conversation with him that'll give me an idea which direction I want to go."

"Oh. I see. Well, let's head on over there." Burrows took his cap down from a peg on the wall and circled his desk to hold the door open for them. "I've heard about the shootings you been having in Bishop's Hill, but I'm 'fraid I haven't had the time to ask around about Inglethorpe the way you wanted. Like I was saying, we've had some excitement of our own here- had a killing over the weekend, and I spent most of yesterday evening with Sheriff Ransome and his men, trying to find out who might've seen or heard anything, and all that."

"Is that so?" replied Talmadge perfunctorily.

"Yes, fellow by the name of Judd Scott was shot to death in his own house. Neighbors say they didn't hear anything out of the ordinary, even though he had his windows open when it happened. His son'd just gotten married about a year ago, and he'd taken to going over to their place for Sunday dinner- his wife left him several years back, and his sister generally did the cooking and cleaning for him. Any rate, when he didn't show up as usual yesterday evening, his boy went on over to look for him, walked into the house and found him lying there dead in the middle of the living room floor with two holes in his stomach."

"Familiar," Sommerlott murmured.

Burrows turned to him curiously, but before he could ask the question that was on his lips Talmadge said, "I'm sure the major'd like to hear the whole story eventually, but right now I want to hear about this man Inglethorpe. What do you know about him?"

"Can't say there's a whole lot to tell. He has five sisters, four of them married. He's something of the black sheep of his family. Works a lot of small jobs here and there around town, for instance he helps out the iceman in the summer, but he hasn't held a steady position anywhere in all the time I've known him."

"He owns his own car?"

"Yes. Well, it's more a family car than anything. His sisters and their husbands use it to go out of town more often than he does, I'd say. After all, the girls did pitch in part of the money to help him get it."

"And he belongs to the K. of P. lodge."

"Yes, his father got him in there. The old man's a respected member of the lodge- and of the community, too. Owns his own business downtown." Burrows shook his head. "Never been quite sure how a man like that managed to have the kind of son he did."

"He won't be expecting us, I hope?"

"No, but we shouldn't have any trouble finding him at home. . . well, you'll see what I mean."

He led them to a large several-gabled house painted in shades of blue. The front door swung open as they started up the walk, and a dark haired young woman stepped out onto the wide porch, having apparently just concluded a conversation with someone inside. She swung her head around at the sound of their footsteps and her brown eyes widened.

Burrows touched the brim of his cap. "Didn't mean to startle you, Miss Inglethorpe. Just come to have a little talk with your brother. This here's Sheriff

Talmadge, from Bishop's Hill, and his friend, Major Sommerlott."

The young woman took a step backwards and her shoulders stiffened. "You want to talk to Jube? Is this- is this something to do with Mr. Scott's dying yesterday?"

"Not as far as I know," Burrows said. "Now why would you think that? No, just a few questions 'bout something else altogether."

"I see. Well, come inside." As she preceded them in she called out, "Jube- Deputy Burrows and some other men to see you."

A voice replied indistinctly from the front of the house. They turned into the living room, where a youngish man with untidy dark brown hair and unshaven jaws was stretched out on the sofa. A faded, shabby dressing gown of blue-and-purple plaid was wrapped around his bony limbs, and a small table with a bowl of fruit on it had been drawn up beside the sofa. He regarded them indifferently with his dull green eyes and continued to champ away at the large apple in his hand.

His left leg, they saw plainly, was encased in a cast that stretched all the way to his hip.

Sheriff Talmadge, without missing a beat, stepped up to him and after introducing himself and shaking his hand said, "That looks to be mighty uncomfortable. How'd it happen?"

"I was working on a friend's shed, replacing some shingles along a corner of the roof, and when I went to climb down my foot missed the ladder, and down I come. Weren't that much a fall, either, that shed ain't that high off the ground, but I landed just right and the bone snapped clean across. Doctor says I'll be stuck with this thing for six weeks."

"Happened recently, did it?"

Inglethorpe narrowed his eyes at the sheriff. "Thursday afternoon. Not long enough for me to get used to the blasted thing yet- and I don't want to, either. What can I do for you?"

Talmadge sat down I an armchair across from him, seemingly at ease. "You've heard about what happened to Perry duBree?"

Inglethorpe nodded. "News gets around 'bout a thing like that. Shot down, wasn't he? In fact, you've been having a stir in your town lately, haven't you? You think I know something 'bout all that?"

"I thought you might be able to tell me a little about duBree. You and he both belonged to the lodge here in Lawrenceville, didn't you?"

"I still do." Behind them Inglethorpe's sister, who had been hovering in the background until she heard the reason for their visit, indicated that she needed to leave, and he nodded at her. "What of it?"

"How well did you know him?"

"We were both members of the lodge, that's all. He was sociable enough, I s'pose, but he wasn't the sort to really make friends with. You know what I mean? Liked to hear himself talk more'n anything else."

"Did you know that he was a blackmailer?"

"Was he? It don't surprise me none."

"Did he ever try to get money out of you?"

Inglethorpe flicked his flat green eyes over the sheriff's face. "No."

"Do you know if he ever tried to blackmail any of your lodge brothers?"

"Nope."

"How about your cousin? You knew he was blackmailing her, didn't you?"

Inglethorpe stared at Talmadge but said nothing.

"Can you tell me where you were Tuesday morning around nine o'clock?"

"I don't see that's any of your business. I ain't done nothing wrong."

Talmadge leaned back in his chair. "Isn't it true that you own a blue car, a 1926 Oakland?"

"And what if I do?"

"A car matching that description," Talmadge said patiently, "was seen in Bishop's Hill Tuesday morning, parked outside Perry duBree's house. That was the day he was killed, in case you weren't aware of it. The man seen driving the car matches your description. How would you like to reconsider your answer?"

Inglethorpe threw his half-eaten apple into the bowl at his elbow and struggled into a more upright position. "Now hold on-"

"D'you keep a pistol in the house?"

"There's a hunting rifle my father give me in the hall closet, and that's all. Now look here-"

"But I'm sure you could borrow a pistol from one of your lodge brothers any time you wanted, couldn't you? Especially if they had an inkling you were going after Perry duBree. . . Do you see your cousin, Celia Durand, very often?"

Inglethorpe's expression was one of complete consternation by that point. "What? No, I haven't seen her in maybe a year or more."

"So she didn't stop in here on her way to the county seat Saturday morning?"

"Of course not."

"And none of your neighbors will remember seeing a little red convertible parked outside your house that morning?"

"If they say so, they're liars."

"You see how it looks, don't you?" Talmadge continued calmly. "Here you knew Perry duBree from your lodge meetings, and your cousin not only had a relationship of sorts with him but was being blackmailed by him, and when he's killed a car that looks like yours is seen outside his house. . ."

"Listen," Inglethorpe said, "I'll tell you exactly where I was Tuesday morning. I remember now, I was splitting wood for Belvidera Hanner. I spent that whole morning out at her place, and she fixed me lunch when I was finished, too. She'll tell you I was there."

Talmadge turned in his chair to look at Deputy Burrows, who had his cap in his hands and was following the conversation with great interest and some puzzlement. "Let me guess- this Mrs. Hanner is up in years?"

"Yessir, eighty-three-year-old widow woman. Sweet as could be, too."

"And the type to not really be sure if it was Tuesday morning when she had this work done, or Wednesday, or Monday? I s'pose," he said to Inglethorpe, "you spent all of Thursday afternoon on your friend's roof, up to when you had your fall?"

"That's right. I been laid up like this since Thursday evening."

"I see. I don't reckon we'll take up any more of your time, then." The sheriff glanced at Major Sommerlott as he rose to his feet, but the major was already settling his hat on his head. "Good day, Mr. Inglethorpe."

The three of them walked back to the jailhouse as slowly as they had come. When they were a distance down the street from the Inglethorpe house Deputy Burrows glanced quizzically at Talmadge and said,

"I don't mean to speak out of turn, but it doesn't seem to me like that conversation got you much of anywhere."

Talmadge shrugged. "Oh, there's no denying I still have plenty of work ahead of me. The first thing I'd like to find out is just where Inglethorpe was this past Tuesday morning –you can be sure he wasn't anywhere near this Mrs. Hanner's- and Tuesday evening, and all day Thursday as well. Then I want to know whether anybody remembers seeing a pistol in his possession recently, or Celia Durand's red convertible outside his house Saturday, and whether any of his lodge brothers noticed that his lodge pin was missing within the past week.

"On the other hand, now that Jube Inglethorpe and Celia Durand know I'm onto them, they're bound to get rattled, and one or the other of 'em may just do something foolish and incriminate themselves."

"Well, I don't know how much poking around Inglethorpe I'm going to be able to do for you. Don't forget, I'm also helping Sheriff Ransome's men look into the killing we've had here."

"The two investigations might well be branches of the same problem," spoke up Major Sommerlott. "You told us, I believe, that your victim was shot twice in the stomach. Perry duBree was murdered in the exact same fashion."

"You think they were killed by the same person? But if Jube Inglethorpe's the man you suspect- why, there's no way he could be involved with the killing of Mr. Scott, not hobbled the way he is, with that cast on his leg."

"It's a possibility that has to be looked into," Talmadge said diplomatically. "You're certain he really has broke his leg?"

"Doc Buell, our town doctor, may be about as old as Methuselah, but I'm pretty sure he still knows a broken leg when he sees one."

"In that case, the real question is when exactly he broke it, and if he had a chance to slip away at all that day. After that it's only a matter of figuring which of them is responsible for which killings."

They had reached the main street by then, and as they crossed toward the jailhouse Deputy Burrows shook his head. "I just don't know what to make of it all. You're talking 'bout a regular murder spree here, aren't you?"

"The simplest way to be certain of the size of the problem before us," Sommerlott said, "would be to compare the bullets that killed your victim –if and when those are recovered- with the bullets that killed Perry duBree and Hall Anglin."

"What's this about bullets, Deputy?"

The speaker was standing on the opposite curb, having just emerged from the town hall. He was a sharp-featured man with a Roman nose and narrow black eyes. He was dressed in a black suit with a red-and-black striped vest and a scarlet tie, and a black snap-brim hat was pushed down over his curly hair. His voice was clipped and businesslike.

"Sheriff Talmadge, I take it?" he asked, extending his hand. "Name's King Kleiner. I'm a special investigator with the sheriff's office- Sheriff Ransome's office, that is." He shook his head, a single movement from side to side. "You people do things a little differently down here, don't you? First county I've ever heard of that had two sheriffs."

"It's an unusual arrangement," Talmadge said, "but not unheard-of, and it's worked out so far. You're not from around these parts, then?"

"No. I imagine my accent gives that away, if nothing else. Maryland, just southeast of Washington, D.C., originally, and a few places since then. . . I hear you've been having some killings down your way, Sheriff."

"Actually," said Major Sommerlott, before Talmadge could respond to this conversational sally, "we'd be more interested in hearing about your victim just now."

"That right? I'm sorry, I didn't catch your name."

Talmadge introduced the major, and explained in a few words his role in the investigation. Kleiner raised his eyebrows.

"A little unorthodox even for your neck of the woods, isn't it?"

Again the sheriff's response was put in abeyance, this time by the arrival of a familiar low roadster in front of the drugstore. Cole Grayson climbed out from behind the wheel and strolled across to them.

"If you've come to find out about Judd Scott," Sommerlott told him, "I'm afraid we're already on that trail. You might as well go on to the county seat and see what you can learn about the last man on the list."

"Can do. By the way, I figured I ought to stop in at the Armstrong farm before I left town. Once I convinced Eb Olsen to point his shotgun somewhere other than at me, he told me there hasn't been anybody suspicious around the place since he's been on guard duty- or much of anybody at all, come to that. Says Burton Armstrong is alive and well and his usual sour self."

"I see."

"I also stopped in at the Jewkes place and had a word with Penny Jewkes and her family. She didn't have anything to add to what she told you and the sheriff the other day. Says she can't remember any visitors to duBree's home other than the ones she named before."

Sommerlott nodded. "Of course, it's always possible that he had visitors at times she wasn't there. His neighbors might be able to tell us more. . . Well, don't let me keep you, Mr. Grayson."

Grayson waved a hand affably at them all and headed back to his car.

"Another one of your investigators, Sheriff?" queried Kleiner.

"Something like that," Talmadge muttered.

"Now," Sommerlott said, "about Judd Scott. . .?"

"Why don't we go and sit down in the jailhouse, and I can go into the details with you?"

Even though it was early yet for lunch, Kleiner sent Deputy Burrows across to the drugstore, and the young man returned with bottles of milk and chicken salad sandwiches wrapped in brown paper. They reclined on the simple wooden chairs in the deputy's office and between bites the sheriff's investigator sketched out what was known in his case so far.

"Scott was forty-one years old, had served in France during the War, worked repairing furniture and upholstery. His wife'd left him six years ago and he lived alone, with his sister coming in from time to time to do some cooking and cleaning for him. No real enemies here in Lawrenceville that anyone can point to. A few grudges here and there, that's normal in a small town, but nothing so far that sounds like it would've led to this. He was killed sometime yesterday afternoon, possibly just after he finished having his lunch, because the kitchen table was only partially cleared. He was seen at church yesterday morning, and far as anyone could tell he didn't appear to have anything particularly on his mind. He'd picked up the habit of taking Sunday dinner with his son and his new bride, and when he didn't show up this time the son went over and found him lying on his back in the middle of the living room floor, shot twice in the stomach. Killer'd taken up one of the pillows from the sofa and fired through it, which explains why none of his neighbors heard the shots on a quiet Sunday afternoon. The attack didn't kill him straight away, though –being gut-shot's a slow and painful way to go- so the killer apparently knelt next to him and held the pillow over his face to finish the job. There was a bit of a struggle –we found blue and purple threads under his fingernails- but he eventually passed out, and the killer threw the pillow back onto the sofa and made his escape. Looks to've slipped out the back way- there were marks of a hard-soled shoe in the sawdust on the floor of Scott's workshop, but none of them complete enough to use as evidence. Front door didn't show any signs of being forced, so it look likes he knew his killer and let him inside willingly, though of course in a small town like this who wouldn't he know?"

"Did you recover the bullets that killed him?" asked Sommerlott.

"Town doctor dug them out of his stomach this morning, and I sent them on by messenger to the State Police post, where they can be properly identified. From the brief look I had at them, they appeared to be from a larger-caliber pistol." Kleiner eyed the major appraisingly. "When I came out of the town hall, you just happened to be discussing bullets with Deputy Burrows here. And you seem to've been looking for Judd Scott, judging from what you said to your man when he arrived. Is there some connection between your investigation and mine that I should be aware of?"

"The major has a theory," Talmadge said carefully, "and that's all it is at this point. I wouldn't want to set you off in the wrong direction with something that hasn't any solid facts behind it yet."

"I appreciate that. But you will let me know if you uncover any definite link between these crimes?"

"Of course." Sheriff Talmadge and Major Sommerlott stood and shook hands with the other two men once more, and took their leave.

On the way back to Bishop's Hill the sheriff, sunk deep in his own thoughts, broke the silence only once. "Burrows," he said, "won't have much time at all to find out what I want to know about Jube Inglethorpe, if he's busy helping Sheriff Ransome's man investigate this other murder. I wonder if it wouldn't be a good idea to put Cole Grayson onto that job instead. . ."

He deposited the major beneath the dogwood tree in front of Shiloah, and Sommerlott spent the remainder of the day immersed in the routine business of his estate. Toward the approach of evening Deputy Anders appeared on his doorstep, cap in hand, and explained that Talmadge wanted him in town once more.

"Cole Grayson's on his way back from the county seat," he relayed, "and the sheriff reckoned you'd want to be there to hear what he has to say."

When Sommerlott entered the sheriff's office he found it in semidarkness. Talmadge had drawn the blind over the single window and was sitting with his long boots crossed on the corner of his desk, mechanically turning a paperweight, a variegated lump of rock a little smaller than his fist, over in his hands. He lifted his head as the other man came through the door.

"Glad you could make it, Major. Make yourself comfortable. I s'pose your day's been fairly quiet?"

"Quiet enough."

In the outer office Deputy Anders had begun pushing a broom across the floor, humming to himself as he went.

"Wish I could say the same thing about mine. Soon's I got back here to my office after our little visit to Lawrenceville I had Marcus Raft call on me, and I had to deal with all his questions- which, I have to admit, are only the same questions everyone hereabouts is asking. This time, though, he had a couple of fellows with him, down from the county seat. Reporters from the *Journal-Dispatch.* I'm afraid the news about these killings is spreading.

"As soon as I'd finished threshing it all out with the three of them the mayor called me into his office, and asked me pretty near the same exact questions. The town council, and the rest of our prominent citizens, want to know how soon I intend to make an arrest, and when they can go back to sleeping soundly at night. I could stand to have something definite to tell them."

He glanced interrogatorily at his visitor, but Sommerlott made no response.

"In the middle of that I was sent for to break up a fight outside the drugstore. One of Mattie Armstrong's older brothers accused another boy, Tollie Hatch, of being the one who shot Mattie, and by the time I got there the two of 'em were rolling around on the ground. There wasn't any real basis for the accusation, of course, just that there'd been bad blood between them for some time and the Hatch boy'd made some vague threats about a week or two before it happened. When they ran into each other outside the drugstore it all come boiling over."

Talmadge shook his head. "Folks're on edge, there's no doubt about that. Three killings and a shooting in the space of a week isn't something you can expect a small town to keep calm about. I surely wouldn't mind being able to tie this thing up nice and quick. . . You wouldn't have any more ideas you'd like to share, would you?"

"Not until I've heard what Mr. Grayson has to say."

"I figured that. That's why I asked Miss Bernetta to let me know if any calls come through from him, so's I could intercept him and hear him make his report the same time as you did. Well, we'll see what he has to tell."

Silence settled on the two men. In the outer office Deputy Anders' broom continued its *whiss-whiss* against the floorboards. Eventually there came the sound of footsteps and voices and Cole Grayson breezed into the room, his suit rumpled and his expression flagging. He exhaled gustily and dropped into the remaining empty chair.

"Bit dark in here, isn't it?" he asked.

Talmadge grunted and sat up, reaching for the cord that opened the slats of the blind. Late afternoon sunlight flooded into the room.

"Well?"

"Well," Grayson returned, "it's been an interesting day, I'll say that much.

"When I got up to the county seat I found that the last man on the major's list, Fred Sears, went and got himself killed this morning in his apartment about two blocks from the square. I got up there about half an hour 'til twelve, and by the time I'd had myself a bite to eat and gotten hold of his address, the police had taken him away and cleared out of the place. If I'd been a mite sooner, I could easily've met them coming out with the body.

"I talked to the widow who owns the building where he lived- something I wouldn't mind doing again, to tell the truth; she's an attractive woman, about forty but easily looks ten years younger. . . At any rate, it turns out her late husband was some distant cousin to Sears, and that's how he come to move into their building. Apparently he was badly injured during the War –the lower half of his face just about blown off, and part of his left ear- and he didn't want folks here, who'd known him all his life, to see him that way. The Army doctors give him a false face to wear, leastways one to cover him from the cheekbones on down, but it was too uncomfortable or awkward or just plain artificial-looking, and he preferred to move somewhere where folks didn't know him, and he could crawl off into a corner and be left alone. And that's what he did. She said he was more or less a recluse; hadn't any visitors she could remember, and the only time he ever left his apartment was in the dead of winter, when he could turn up his collar and wrap a muffler 'round the bottom half of his face and look more or less like a normal person, and then he'd go walking from one end of the city to the other, never mind how cold it got. Didn't generally seem as though he talked to anybody on these walks of his, just took the fresh air and exercise and sometimes bought a paper. Not as though he could really make himself understood, either, with his injuries. I s'pose it helped him keep from going stir-crazy.

"She said she and her husband were the only ones he ever let into his rooms, and the only ones he ever showed his uncovered face to. Said the first time she saw it it give her the screaming meemies, the mangled, raw skin and the odd way it moved 'cause of the damage to the jawbone and muscles, and she had to keep her hand over her mouth the whole time so she wouldn't cause a scene. But eventually she got used to it, and by the time her husband died she could understand Sears' talk clear as anything.

"Then this morning out of the blue he had a visitor, the first time she knew that to happen in all the years he'd lived there. It was a man, on the tall side and she thought dark-headed, but she couldn't be sure 'cause he kept his hat pulled down low and avoided looking her in the eye. He asked if Fred Sears was in, and was it the same room he'd always had, and she said yes, 3A, and the man thanked her and went on up. She was in the middle of cleaning house when this man come to the door of her apartment, and she figured she was still at it when he left, 'cause she didn't see him go. When she carried Sears' lunch up to him as usual later on –he had a special diet, had to have soft foods or else his meat and vegetables cut into tiny pieces- there wasn't any response to her knock. The door wasn't bolted when she tried it, either, which wasn't usual, so she knocked again and marched right in –and found Fred Sears sitting in his armchair with a belt wrapped around his neck.

"She's a strong woman, I'll say that for her. She took one look at him, enough to know he was good and dead, set the tray she'd brought up down on the nearest table calm as you please, went out and locked the door behind her, and went down to the 'phone in the entryway and called for the police. Then and only then did she sit down and have herself a nice little case of the hysterics. She was still a bit shaky when I talked to her, but she told her story clear enough.

"After I'd talked to her I set about trying to talk to his neighbors, but none of them claimed to've seen or heard anything out of the ordinary. At least one of them must've thought I seemed a trifle suspicious, asking around the way I was, especially after they'd just got through answering the same questions to the police, because when I stepped out of the apartment house afterward two men were waiting for me on the sidewalk. They took ahold of my arms, one on each side, hustled me into a car waiting at the curb, and drove me straight 'round to the police station. Turned out they were two of Chief Kearns' plainclothes men, and he and his lieutenant ran me through the paces most of the afternoon. What was I doing poking my nose into an official investigation?

How did I know Fred Sears? Where was I when he was killed? Finally they decided somebody as winsome as myself couldn't possibly have anything to do with what happened to him, and they let me go-though you'll probably be getting a 'phone call from one of Chief Kearns' men about me at some point."

Talmadge nodded. "Already have. Kearns himself called here about half an hour before they decided to cut you loose. I told him I could vouch for you, but I wouldn't have any definite information to give him 'til after I'd talked to you. Did he seem to think his murder's connected to the ones here?"

Major Sommerlott, who was clearly following another train of thought entirely, asked, "Sheriff, do you happen to have those lists you were telling us about yesterday?"

Talmadge opened one of his desk drawers with a frown and handed across the two sheets of paper, then turned back expectantly to Cole Grayson. Sommerlott glanced over the typed pages and nodded to himself.

"Well now," Grayson responded, quirking up one side of his mouth ironically, "I wouldn't exactly say the chief and I had a heart-to-heart parley. More like they asked the questions, and I answered them. But no, overall I'd guess they haven't any interest in what's been happening here. They only asked me about Fred Sears, not about anything outside of that."

"I'm not too surprised." Talmadge at last gave up toying with his paperweight and returned it to its usual place. "From what you've told us, it's pretty obvious Jube Inglethorpe hadn't anything to do with this killing up at the county seat, and it seems to me the same's true of the killing in Lawrenceville."

"You don't believe, then," Sommerlott asked quietly, "that Judd Scott was murdered by the person who murdered Perry duBree, despite the similarity of method?"

"If all I have to go on is two shots to the belly, then I'm going to have to say no, I don't think there's the same hand behind both of them. I know the sheriff's man, Kleiner, found purple and blue threads under his victim's fingernails, and Jube Inglethorpe was wearing a purple-and-blue robe when we saw him, but d'you really reckon he stumped over there with that cast on his leg, wearing a robe instead of regular clothes, and shot Judd Scott to death? In the first place, how would he've managed to kneel next to the victim and hold a pillow over his face, the way Kleiner said the killer did? More importantly, how could he've gotten there and back without being noticed and recognized by half the town?

"And if I assume Celia Durand carried out that particular killing, then the evidence doesn't fit. You can be sure if the footprint they found in the back of Scott's house'd belonged to a woman's shoe, Kleiner would've said so. I don't imagine for a minute he'd miss something as obvious as that.

"The killing up at the county seat's even easier to rule out. That widow woman Cole talked to didn't say a single word about her mysterious visitor having one leg in a cast, and that'd be the sort of detail a body wouldn't soon forget, no matter how upset she was afterwards. Besides, did Inglethorpe look to you like a man who'd just driven up to the county seat, committed a murder, and driven back again? He didn't to me. I'd take an oath he hadn't moved from that couch all morning. Or am I s'posed to figure Celia Durand drove up there to kill Fred Sears dressed as a man? You really think that pretty little girl could've masqueraded as a tall man and gotten away with it, especially in front of another woman? And why, in the name of all that's holy, would she've wanted to?"

Talmadge shook his head, half defensively and half in irritation. "Major, I appreciate you've got a sort of theory you'd like to fit all this into, but don't you see that dragging in those last two killings throws the whole thing out of joint? Without them it all hangs together. Celia Durand and Jube Inglethorpe working in tandem had the means, the motive, and the opportunity. Tuesday morning, while she gets up a solid alibi for herself, Inglethorpe drives down here and kills Perry duBree. Then, two days later, he does the same with Hall Anglin. Remember, he didn't break his leg 'til late in the day Thursday. Friday afternoon, when Inglethorpe is laid up with his leg in a cast and wouldn't've been able to get into Mrs. Brett's boardinghouse without being noticed, Celia Durand sneaks in and kills Marcel Carr. As for which of them drove past the Armstrong place and shot young Mattie, I haven't made up my mind yet. She could've driven her cousin's car to do it –we only have her word she was up at the county seat all that day, and a pile of packages that could've been bought anytime- or maybe Inglethorpe did it himself. It would've been some kind of feat to operate a car with one leg in a cast, but I won't say such a thing's impossible.

"Speaking of Hall Anglin, one of his neighbors told me he saw a car parked in Anglin's front yard when he drove past there Thursday afternoon, and Anglin and another man standing by it talking. He wasn't sure of the color of the car, just that it was dark, but what d'you want to bet it was blue?

"And I'm sure you're itching to remind me of Paul Turner's disappearing, Major, but until I find out more about him I won't know for certain what he has to do with all this. More'n likely he cleared out for reasons of his own. 'Course I s'pose he could've been killed too, but so far I haven't any evidence to make me think so."

"Mind if I put forward a possibility, Sheriff?" asked Grayson. Talmadge shrugged and sat back in his chair. "If I follow your idea right, the killer's someone who drives a blue car and has some connection both with Lawrenceville and with Perry duBree's victims- one of 'em being Oliver Parrish. Well, I happen to know Parrish's sister is engaged to a fellow from Lawrenceville by the name of Billy Scobell, who drives a blue automobile." He leaned sideways and scanned the papers in Major Sommerlott's hand. "Yes, you have him down here- William Scobell, owns a 1925 Studebaker Six. If Celia Durand and this Inglethorpe character don't pan out as suspects, you might consider Parrish and Scobell. There's no telling, with them you might be able to string all these killings together."

Talmadge, only half-listening, was studying Sommerlott's face. "You don't think I'm on the right trail, do you, Major? You don't think Jube Inglethorpe is the man I'm after –or Billy Scobell. Who, then?"

Sommerlott shook his head. "I have nearly everything," he said, "except proof, and without that there's no point in naming names. The chain of reasoning that I've followed might be convincing to me, but it wouldn't suffice in a court of law. What we need-"

He turned to Grayson and briefly gave him directions in a low tone, while the sheriff leaned forward, resting his weight on his forearms. Cole Grayson sat bolt upright in his chair.

"Major, you're surely fooling. You don't suspect him of being involved in these killings!"

"Let me ask you something," Sommerlott said thoughtfully. "When you spoke with him yesterday, what was he wearing?"

Grayson narrowed his eyes in recollection. "Earlier in the day, you mean? He had on a brown suit. . . no, I'm wrong, he had on a charcoal grey suit."

"And his necktie?"

Grayson's eyes went wide. "A blue tie with violet stripes. . . Major, it has to be a coincidence. That's all there is to it."

"If only it were. But someone has to be culpable of these crimes."

He gave the young man some further instructions, while the sheriff listened with a frown. "Hopefully we'll be able to uncover the proof we need before he has a chance to act again. Because, unless I'm very much mistaken, he's making plans for another murder even now."

CHAPTER TEN

Tuesday, May 19, 1931

So Joab went in to the king and said, "What have you done?"

-2 Samuel 3:24

Major Sommerlott turned in at the gate reluctantly and climbed with a heavy tread up the steps to the front porch. In the morning sunlight his surroundings had a crispness and clarity about them, as well as a certain sense of expectation, as of a theater stage where the curtain has just been drawn back but the machinery of the play has not yet been set in motion. There was little activity along the street, although windows and doors were thrown open here and there; only the birds in the treetops were already long busy. Surely, he thought, it was not too early to call.

Pray the Lord it wasn't already too late.

He gave the bell-pull several sharp twists. The inner door of the house stood open, but the hallway beyond was unilluminated, so that when an outline eventually loomed up on the other side of the screen he had no way of telling who it was. It was of course the manservant, who even at that hour was immaculate, with his starched white shirt and pressed trousers. He held the screen door open, his smooth dark face impassive as always, and murmured,

" 'Morning, Major. If you'll just step in here, suh, I'll let Mist' Hitchens know you're here. . . Am I allowed to ask, suh, the reason for this morning's visit?"

"Mr. Hitchens will know why I'm calling."

"Yassuh," the servant said doubtfully, and returned shortly with the pronouncement: "He's in the summer room, suh. This way. . ."

He led Sommerlott directly through to the back of the house. The "summer room" was a little nook opening off the kitchen, with a row of windows along its longer wall to catch the sunlight and create a cheerful corner in which to enjoy breakfast or play a hand of cards after dinner. Frank Hitchens was seated at a small table inside it, with his empty dishes in front of him and a copy of the day's newspaper open in his hands.

"Thank you, Vernon," he said as his man gathered up the dishes. "That'll be all. In fact, I don't believe we'll be needing you again until dinnertime, so you may consider yourself at liberty until then. Er-leave my cup, there's a good fellow. Now, won't you have a seat, Major?" Hitchens gestured at the cushioned chairs spaced about the room. "I can spare you a few minutes before I have to be downtown. Vernon said something about you saying that I'd know why you were calling. I take it that means you're following up on your last visit, and you're still hoping I can tell you something that'll help along the sheriff's investigation?"

"I'm certain of it now. I have an almost complete picture of the circumstances surrounding these killings, and I wanted to speak to you once more before I laid the facts I have before the sheriff, in the hope that you could clear up a few remaining points."

"I can't say I have any real idea what makes you think I'd have the answers you're looking for, unless it's that business about my being in the same squad as the victims during the War. And that seems a pretty thin connection to me. No, I haven't changed my opinion any since the last time we talked. I still maintain the culprit's someone who was being blackmailed by Perry duBree, and decided to take the law into his own hands." Hitchens folded his paper and threw it down, then pushed his chair back from the little table. "I'm going to have myself another cup of coffee, Major. Care for one yourself?"

"No, thank you." Sommerlott squeezed back out of the nook and followed his host into the kitchen. Hitchens was standing at the cabinets along the far wall with his back to him, fiddling with milk and cream, and Sommerlott pulled out the chair at the end of the kitchen table and sat down.

Without turning around Hitchens asked, "Now when you said you have more or less the whole picture on these killings, you weren't exaggerating, were you? You're telling me you know who the killer is?"

"Yes. The murderer is someone of roughly my age or yours, a man with dark hair and the same general build as Perry duBree, who drives a blue automobile. He also belonged to the same Army squad that duBree and Marcel Carr belonged to- and that you belonged to, Mr. Hitchens. Beginning this past Tuesday, he has killed one man a day –with a single exception- sometimes in the morning, sometimes in the evening. That part of his scheme I'll confess I haven't made sense of."

Hitchens leaned back against the cabinet counter and sipped on his coffee, regarding his guest thoughtfully. "So you have no doubt all of these attacks are connected?"

"None."

"And you have proof of who's behind this?"

"I do."

"It sounds, then," Hitchens said slowly, "like there's only one part of the picture you're missing."

"Precisely. There's one question that I don't yet know the answer to: Why?"

Major Sommerlott pulled from his pocket a damp, soiled ribbon of fabric, medium blue with thin, diagonal, violet stripes, rent in several places, and dropped it onto the tabletop.

"Why did you kill those men, Mr. Hitchens?"

Hitchens stopped with his cup halfway to his mouth, then lowered it without saying a word. He eyed his visitor narrowly.

"Cole Grayson found this where you buried it, at the bottom of the trash barrel at the edge of your property. He also informed me that there's a scratch down the passenger side of your car –your blue Essex Coach- and it should be simple enough to match it to the blue paint on the brass buttons of the coat Perry duBree was wearing when he died. Not to mention that the bullets recovered from certain of the victims can be matched to the pistol that was used, which you no doubt still have here in your house, and that the landlady of Fred Sears' apartment house will have no trouble identifying his visitor of yesterday morning. . ."

Hitchens shook his head. "I thought I heard some noises outside late last night, but I told myself it was just stray dogs scratching around. Appears I've been a little too sure of myself. . . The sheriff knows all about this, too, I s'pose?"

"I haven't presented all of the evidence to him yet. I thought- I thought I owed you a chance to tell your side of the story first."

"You'd like to know what's been back of it all, is that it?"

Frank Hitchens looked hard at his visitor for a moment longer, then abruptly appeared to come to some decision and drained his cup, setting it down beside him on the countertop.

"Do you remember Camp Jackson, Major? Where we were sent for training before being shipped overseas to the front? Of course you do- I don't know why I'm asking. And you'll remember that while we recruits were responsible for keeping our own barracks clean, the officers always had someone to do their cleaning for them, generally from somewhere lower down the ranks. The camp commander, on the other hand, had an old colored fellow who came in from outside to look after his quarters.

"This old Sambo of the commander's lived with his woman and her daughter in a little shack at the end of a narrow lane just outside the camp. I say old, but looking back he was probably only in his fifties- just far enough along to have some grey hairs coming in on his woolly head. He'd married a woman some twenty years younger than him, and not only that, but apparently she'd been with a white man at some point. We used to see them together sometimes on their porch on our way back from town, or occasionally when one or the other of the women brought a message to him in the camp, and it only took one look to realize the girl wasn't his blood. He was black as pine tar at midnight himself, and his wife was dark enough, though she wasn't bad-looking for a Negress, but that girl- only sixteen or seventeen at most, creamy skin just a shade too dusky to ever pass for white, large hazel eyes, curly reddish-brown hair, thick sensuous mouth. . . and too callow to show any sense about how she behaved around the soldiers she saw every day- or maybe just too headstrong to care, I don't know. When she got wolf whistles and bawdy suggestions, why, she'd just flash her teeth and flirt right back, the little tramp. I don't imagine she ever let her folks catch her carrying on that way, though, or they'd've put an end to it quick enough.

"It all came to a head on the night before we shipped out. The curfew'd been extended for that one night for just that reason, to let us blow off some steam and enjoy the comforts of home one last time;

the brass knew full well some of us wouldn't ever be seeing home again.

"Our squad drove into town and hit the night spots like all the rest, with Perry duBree at the vanguard. He was our squad leader, after all, besides being the sort who expects everyone else to fall in line with his every whim and notion. We were headed back to camp at the end of the evening, with a good sight more brew in us than usual, when we reached the lane running up to this colored man's shack and saw that there were still lights burning in the windows. DuBree, who was at the wheel of the car we'd borrowed, immediately turned and started us up the lane.

"I'll say this, I don't think what happened then would've happened if we hadn't all been drinking- but that's neither here nor there.

"He cut the engine a little distance from the shack and hissed at us to follow him and keep quiet, and we climbed out and passed the rest of the way on foot. In the August heat every single window in the place stood open, and even though the lamps were turned down low we could see the family clearly as we approached. They were sitting around the parlor, the old man with a newspaper in his hands, the mother and daughter with a pile of knitting between them on the shabby couch. It seems incredible to me that in that stillness they didn't hear the sound of our boots tramping along the path up to their shack, but it was a hot, drowsy sort of evening, and so. . . I don't doubt that old spade had a squirrel gun or some such thing tucked away in that cabin somewhere, and if he'd managed to get to it the situation might've turned out a bit different. . .

"DuBree padded up to the front door, threw it open and stepped inside, with the rest of us crowding in behind him. In the state we were in by that point I imagine we'd probably have followed him just about anywhere. That old colored man lifted his head from his newspaper and opened his mouth to protest, but the words just sort of died off in his throat, and the two women froze there on the couch where they were, with their arms wrapped around each other and their eyes wide as saucers. DuBree started barking orders at us: to grab the nigras and keep them quiet, to scout around for some rope, that it was time for us to get a piece of that colored tail that'd been paraded 'round in front of us for too long. He dragged a chair in from the kitchen, tied the old man's hands behind him and a gag over his mouth and forced him up onto the chair, and then looped the rest of the rope we'd dug out over one of the beams of the ceiling and dropped it down around his neck.

"And then he had us draw all the curtains, and we started in on the women.

"There's no need for me to describe for you what went on that night in that shack, Major. You can imagine it well enough for yourself. The two women struggled, bit, pleaded, prayed, but there wasn't anything they could do against the twelve of us, and all they got for their trouble was one blow after another.

"Perry duBree took his turn first, of course, and when he'd finished he stood over us and watched to make sure we did the same. Drunk as I was I could see how it was going to end, and when I'd had my turn I mumbled something about standing guard and staggered out onto the porch. Even now I can recall how thick and still that night air was, not the tiniest bit of a breeze to stir the drops of sweat on my skin. Finally, when the sounds from inside the shack'd tapered off, I opened the door again and looked in. The two women were sprawled across the floor at unnatural angles, their clothes torn to shreds and their bodies bruised from head to foot, and by their glazed expressions I knew they were dead or well on their way. Meanwhile the old buck stood quivering on his chair, his eyes clenched shut and water rolling down his black cheeks. As I watched from the threshold duBree hitched his thumbs under his belt, glanced around him at the wreckage of the room, and then with a sneer kicked the chair out from under the old man.

"By the time we pulled 'round to the camp gates it was past curfew, and we got bawled out for that, but the commander's only real concern by then was to make sure we were on the train for Newport

News the next morning. Apart from Perry duBree, who never had a lick of tact in his whole life, we never talked about what'd happened that night among ourselves, and I can't remember ever hearing it referred to by any other man who'd been at Camp Jackson. I don't s'pose you heard any rumor of it yourself at the time, did you, Major?. . . The authorities probably figured, when they eventually found the bodies, that the old man'd killed his wife and stepdaughter himself, and then hanged himself in remorse. . .

"After the War ended I saw the survivors of my original squad around town, of course, but I didn't go out of my way to have dealings with them. Perry duBree didn't make any attempts to chisel money out of me then, though he'd apparently already started in with his blackmailing tricks, and he ended up moving to Columbia not too long after.

"By the time he worked his way back down here again some things had changed. In the intervening years I'd taken the few business holdings my father left me, built them up and added to them with good old-fashioned horse sense, and become a successful merchant, a well-respected member of the community. And a likely prospect to someone like duBree.

"Of course he was up to the same old schemes. Shortly after he moved back he just 'happened' to run across me on the square, and asked if I wouldn't mind dropping by his home for a chat. I visited him twice, while he spun me a yarn about a business opportunity that'd come his way. He suggested perhaps I'd be willing to advance him some funds for this venture, seeing as how we'd been through the War together, and especially in view of old times. I confess I didn't immediately grasp what he meant by that latter remark. By my second visit I'd heard enough to turn down his proposition in no uncertain terms, and that's when he made his meaning clear. He implied that he had in his possession a written statement signed by some of the members of our old squad, describing what'd happened that night in 1917 and naming names, and if I were willing to part with certain regular sums he'd make sure that statement stayed hidden away from prying eyes. Considering my position in the community, he said, I had the most to lose if the facts came to light, and I could certainly afford the cost of his silence.

"I made him some sharp reply at that and stormed out of his house, but he wasn't one to give up so easily. He showed up here a few days later to ask whether I'd reconsidered my position. As a matter of fact I'd been doing quite a bit of thinking in the meantime, and I told him I'd come to his house the following day with my answer.

"I'll tell you the God's honest truth, I didn't sleep hardly at all that night. It's a heavy thing, to realize you have a great responsibility weighing on your shoulders, that you're the only one who can act. The fact of the matter is, every man in our squad had a share in what happened that night fourteen years ago, but there was no way the authorities were going to lift a finger to bring any of us to account for it. If there was going to be any justice this side of Kingdom Come, it wouldn't be a court or a military tribunal that'd bring it. I knew what had to be done, and it was up to me to do it, and no one else.

"I met Perry duBree in front of his house the next morning –this was last Tuesday, of course- and suggested we take a drive out away from curious eyes and ears and work out an arrangement. He was so blamed greedy and so all-fired sure of himself that it never occurred to him it might be a bad idea to climb into a car with a man he was trying to blackmail."

"The sheriff wondered," Sommerlott said, "why you took the chance of having your vehicle recognized, pulling up to his house in broad daylight as you did. Why not simply arrange to meet duBree in a secluded location in the first place?"

"I'll grant you it was a risk, but not nearly as much of a one as you might imagine. I so rarely drive my own car, you see –when I have business to tend to around town I nearly always walk, and for special occasions we use Henry's roadster to get around- so I didn't figure there was much danger of it being recognized. And it wasn't, either, far as I'm aware.

Besides, I didn't want to immediately put duBree on his guard by suggesting some out-of-the-way rendezvous.

"I drove out along the Merom Road, making idle conversation meantime, and stopped the car in a secluded stretch about a quarter-mile from where the old Ivie farm used to be. I told him I had something to show him, and as I climbed out of the car I took my gun out from under my seat, where I'd stashed it earlier. My old service revolver, appropriately enough. By the time I came 'round to his side of the car he'd climbed out as well, and when he opened his mouth to demand an explanation I shot him. I dragged his body out of sight among the trees, and took his ring of keys off him before I left. That night, after it was good and dark, I used the keys to get into his house and into the safe he'd had installed under his stairs, where he kept his blackmail grist. He'd shown me his workroom there the very first time I visited him; the photographic equipment, the safe, all of it. Bragged about it, even. Can you picture the cocksureness of the man?. . . Fortunately the safe was one of the cheaper variety, that only needed a key to open it. I scooped up every paper and photograph in his lockbox, not bothering to fetch out the particular one he'd threatened me with, and hid the lot under my coat. When I got home I started up my car and drove down to the Savannah, where I tied the whole mess into a packet, weighted it down with a rock, and threw it in. That's the last anybody'll ever see of Perry duBree's handiwork, I'll wager."

"You also returned his hat to his home during your visit. . ."

Hitchens regarded his guest keenly. "Is there any detail you don't notice, Major? Yes, when I returned home from that little jaunt into the countryside Tuesday morning, I was unpleasantly surprised to glance over and see his hat lying there on the passenger seat of my car. In my preoccupation with disposing of him I'd failed to perceive that he was bareheaded when I shot him down. I did the only thing I could think to do, and left the hat there while I went off to work, expecting no one in my household would have any reason to go looking inside my car- or if they did, that they'd simply assume it was one of mine. That night, when I went to his home, I wore it instead of my own and left it hanging on his coat tree. It sat halfway down over my ears, but in the dark who'd be likely to make out a thing like that?

"The next day I went after Paul Turner. By then I'd worked it all out in my mind, and it seemed reasonable to go after them one at a time –one per day, that is- and I expected to be able to reach all seven of them before anyone caught on to what was happening. I hadn't reckoned on your taking an interest in the investigation. . . Turner was a notorious gambler, and usually frequented the roadhouse out at Hobb's End. I don't s'pose you know anything much about the place, do you, Major? They've fixed up an old farmhouse with poker tables and dancing and half a dozen other things, and on the weekends especially the field next to it is packed with cars. I parked my own car up a deserted lane a little ways past there around midnight –a lovers' lane, only not on a weekday night, of course- and walked back. I'd figured to have to wait some time before I caught sight of Turner, but as a matter of fact I'd been standing in the shadows near his car for not even an hour when he stepped outside. I walked up to him as he was leaned over filling his cigarette case, and handed him some talk about needing someone to drive me back up the road and help me patch a flat tire. He eventually agreed, though I first had to convince him we didn't need to fetch a couple of his friends along to help. When he pulled his car in behind mine I took my revolver from my pocket and shot him like I'd shot Perry duBree, twice in the stomach, with the gun held in close so's it'd make less noise. Not that there was ever much danger of my attracting attention; with all the music and merrymaking going on at the roadhouse the chances were nil anybody there'd hear the shots, and any decent folk who lived out that way'd long since gone to bed. I dragged his body across to my side of the car and circled 'round and got behind the wheel. I drove the car further up the lane, near where it peters out in an empty field, and pushed it in among the trees and brush as far as I could. Turner was moving around, trying to work his door open, so I clubbed him over the head with the butt of my gun to stop him struggling, and then I piled loose branches and such – whatever I could reach in the dark- over the car to hide it from sight and drove home.

"The following morning you and Henry discovered Perry duBree's carcass, and by the afternoon the story was all over town. When I drove out to Hall Anglin's place, though, I found the grapevine hadn't reached as far as him yet. I ended up being the one to break the news to him. He was just coming out of that shack of his when I pulled up into his yard, about to head into town, and we stood there and talked for a bit. He claimed he hadn't spoken to duBree since he'd moved back to Bishop's Hill and hadn't any interest in what he'd been up to, and he may well've been telling the truth- not that it mattered all that much. When he turned towards his truck I slipped my revolver from my pocket and followed him, and when he climbed inside I put it against his head and pulled the trigger. Afterward I scouted 'round to make sure I hadn't left any footprints behind and got the blazes out of there.

"On Friday afternoon I paid a visit to Marcel Carr. I know what time they generally have supper there at Mrs. Brett's, and I knew Carr rarely ventured out of his room, so I slipped in there about a quarter 'til six, when the household would be gathering in the back yard to wash up and I'd have a chance to catch him. I realized I probably wouldn't be able to shoot him without the whole house hearing me, so instead I brought a length of rope in my pocket to do the job. When I stepped into his room and spied that heavy clock sitting on his bureau, though, it struck me that that'd be an even better solution. Why use something that might lead back to me some way when I had the means already at my fingertips? I told him Perry duBree's death had worried me and gotten me to thinking about our old Army days, and when he turned to get something off his writing table I snatched up the clock with both hands and brought it down on his head. In the process I spattered blood on my hands and cuffs, so after I fished the key to his room from his pocket I stopped and used his washbasin to wash up. Then I folded my coat over my arm to keep the bloodstains out of sight, and when I'd made sure the coast was clear I wriggled out into the hallway. As small as his room was, with him stretched out dead across the floor like that there was hardly space to get the door open. I locked the door behind me to give myself a chance to get away before the body was found and then kicked the key back under it- no sense in carrying it away with me, like I'd done with Perry duBree's hat- and headed downstairs. On the way out I was stopped by Mrs. Brett, and I had to go through the rigmarole of accompanying her back up to Carr's room to see if he was in. For a moment I was afraid she'd use her own key to open his door, and then there'd be a dead body to explain. But when she found the door was locked she just assumed he'd had to step out for some reason, and I was able to get away with nobody the wiser.

"The next day I had an early lunch and drove out to the Armstrong farm to try and work out how I was going to get at Burton Armstrong. Of course there was a risk in my doing that, as well, but he tends to stay around their property most of the time, and so I knew my opportunities there would be limited, and I'd need to know the lay of the land. But as I was driving by I saw someone I thought was Burton standing in the garden in front of the house. It felt like fate was smiling down on me. I grabbed my revolver quickly from under my seat –where I'd stashed it just exactly in case such a chance presented itself- and fired through the passenger window. It's a wonder I wounded the boy only as much as I did; it takes the devil's own luck to fire one-handed from a moving vehicle with any accuracy. I was sorry when I eventually learned I'd shot Burton's nephew by mistake, I really was; I haven't any ill will against the boy or his people.

"On Sunday afternoon I drove into Lawrenceville to the home of Judd Scott. After the hash I'd made of things the day before, I took my time and was as careful as I could be. I parked my car in a side street a few blocks away, beside a warehouse, and walked back, trying my best to look nonchalant. There was still a danger of my being seen and remembered, of course, but not nearly as much as if I'd parked directly in front of his house. I hadn't seen him in several years, and he invited me in cordial as you please. We stood and talked for a few minutes in his living room about this and that, and then I picked up one of the pillows off his sofa, took my pistol from my pocket, and fired through it. It was a good thing I did, too- with his windows open the way they were, the sound of a pistol shot would've carried otherwise and brought all the neighbors running. Then I held the pillow over his face until he stopped moving, and slipped out the back door and around the side of the house. I'd meant to take a moment or two before I went to make certain I hadn't left any incriminating traces behind, and to be sure nobody'd see me go, but I heard a noise that made me think someone was at the front door, and so I hurried and got out of there. There wasn't anybody in sight when I reached the street, though.

"Yesterday morning I drove up to the county seat and hunted down Fred Sears. He lived in an apartment building near the center of town, and I again brought that coil of rope in my pocket, to deal with him as noiselessly as possible. I tried to keep the landlady of his building from getting a good look at me, but it sounds as if I didn't quite pull it off. When

I knocked at his door and told him who it was, he let me in without hesitation and immediately started in talking about the members of our old squad. He was the only one of the seven who had any idea at all of what'd really been happening with these killings. He hadn't a thing to do all day but sit in his apartment, you see, reading the newspapers and listening to the radio and putting two and two together. Soon as he'd settled himself into his usual armchair with his back to me I took hold of the rope in my pocket, but then I caught sight of his belt hanging across the corner of his bedpost and reached for that instead. It seemed fitting somehow to kill him with that. It wasn't near as noisy or difficult as I'd figured it would be, to strangle him. I was sure he'd put up more of a fight than he did. In a way I wonder if, once he'd guessed what was coming, he didn't almost welcome it- after all, what kind of a life could that've been, with his face more than half blasted away, no real chance of having a family to call his own, staying boxed up in that apartment year round? I slipped out quietly as I could after it was done; I'd thought of locking the door behind me the way I'd done with Marcel Carr, but there were no keys in any of his pockets and I didn't think I'd better stay around long enough to search further.

"Well, Major, I trust I've explained it all to your satisfaction? I haven't left any questions unanswered? . . . You can see why I had to take the course I did, even after all this time, to deal with what was done all those years ago at Camp Jackson? Someone had to bring judgement down on them, even if the victims were only an old colored man and his family, to see that justice was done, when the law would only have washed its hands of them. . ."

"You've explained yourself very clearly, Mr. Hitchens," Sommerlott said quietly.

"All that talking made me right parched, if I do say so. I believe I'll have myself another cup of coffee. Will you join me, Major? You take yours black, isn't that so? To be honest, I can't see how you can stand to drink it that way. I always have to have plenty of milk and sugar in mine. . ."

"If it isn't any trouble," Sommerlott murmured, "I suppose I could have just one cup. . ."

Hitchens had turned away by then and appeared not to have heard him. He began to rattle about with cups and pitchers, spoons and sugar bowl, humming lightly to himself, while the major stared thoughtfully at his broad back and drummed his fingertips on the tabletop.

Hitchens abruptly broke off his humming at the sound of a knock at the front door. His shoulders went stiff, and he stepped slowly back from the kitchen cabinets in order to see clearly down the length of the house. Just visible in the shade of the front porch, blurred a bit by the intervening screen door, was a tall figure with a flat-brimmed hat and a six-pointed star pinned to his breast.

In an oddly flat voice he said: "John Talmadge is standing on my front porch."

Sommerlott nodded. "I asked him to meet me here as soon as he was able."

The sheriff pounded on the front door again. Hitchens swung around to meet his guest, his right hand clenched and his black eyes shining.

"With a warrant for my arrest, no doubt? Major, did you really think I'd let this end that way? Honestly imagine for a minute that I'd let myself be arrested, led off in chains and put on trial?"

In that instant, as Major Sommerlott realized that the businessman's right hand was not balled into a fist but was clutching something, Hitchens raised his hand to his mouth and drank.

"No!" Sommerlott shouted and shot to his feet, sending his chair over backwards with a clatter. Hitchens began to cough harshly, a series of sharp barks that bent him nearly in two, and his eyes squeezed shut. The object he had been holding in his hand dropped to the floor and rolled against the base of the cabinets.

At the major's cry the sheriff flung open the screen door and came running, his boots pounding along the polished hallway. By the time he reached the kitchen Frank Hitchens was stretched out on the floor, his body convulsing violently and his face a dreadful bluish-grey color. Sommerlott was kneeling beside him, struggling unsuccessfully to loosen his collar and necktie.

"We have to get Doctor Van Allen!" the major said hoarsely. From somewhere the manservant, Vernon, had appeared in the kitchen doorway, his eyes protruding whitely from his face and his mouth hanging open, and Sommerlott staggered toward him on his knees. "For God's sake, man, go for the telephone!"

"It's too late, Major," Talmadge said thickly, as the businessman's convulsions ceased suddenly and a final arching spasm pushed the remaining air from his lungs with a ghastly sigh. "It's over. He's dead."

CHAPTER ELEVEN

Tuesday, May 19, 1931

Who is wise, that he may understand these things?
Discreet, that he may know them?

-Hosea 14:9

Talmadge took a deep breath, pushed open the screen door, and stepped out onto the back porch. Major Sommerlott was sitting about halfway down the porch steps, his shoulders hunched, staring sightlessly out across the length of the Hitchens property.

The sheriff walked over and down the steps and sat down beside him with a sigh. He held out the other man's straw hat, which had been left hanging on a peg in the front hall. The major took it silently, without turning his head.

"Van Allen's helping Wardin Gates –the undertaker- load the body onto his wagon now. He says there wasn't a single thing you or I could've done to help Hitchens, not with what he took and the way he took it." Talmadge held up the small brown-glass bottle he had recovered from the kitchen floor. The label pasted to its front bore an oversize skull and crossbones. "Corrosive sublimate solution. Used as a preservative, oddly enough, and deadly poison. They sell the stuff at the hardware store- Hitchens could've pocketed a bottle of it the last time he visited the back offices there. He swallowed pretty near the whole bottle, and with it going straight into his system the way it did. . ."

The back door opened and Deputy Christie poked his head out. "Sheriff, Mr. Gates wants a word with you."

Sommerlott stood abruptly and faced the other man, settling his hat on his head with unsteady fingers. His eyes were haunted. "Sheriff, I- I need to get away from here. I imagine you have certain things to take care of yet before you'll be finished here, but when you're ready to ask the questions you have for me- and I have no doubt you have questions- you'll find me at the Noultons'. It isn't far. . . isn't very far from here. . ."

Talmadge nodded. "I'll let your boy know where you've gone, Major."

Sommerlott walked the three blocks to the home of the Noulton family nervelessly, with the stiff gait of a somnambulist. The news had begun to spread already and people streamed past him, drawn like flies, eager to view the scene of this latest tragedy with their own eyes; several of them made as if to call out to him, but when they saw the expression on his face they held their tongues. Upon reaching his destination he started up the path to the front porch the same as any other visitor, but he heard voices coming from the rear of the house and veered around to knock on the back door.

The Noulton home was small and cozy, painted brick red and framed in viburnum and hollyhock: in short, a place where a person might readily feel at ease. Mrs. Noulton, who opened the door to him, was curly-headed and plump, resembling her daughter in height and coloration, and similarly cheerful. Her eyes widened when she saw their visitor.

"Why, Major Sommerlott! Land of Goshen, what's happened now? You look all out. Come in, come in, sit right down here."

The back door opened directly onto their boxlike kitchen. The smell of bacon and eggs hung in the air, and Mrs. Noulton, a flowered apron wrapped around her middle, was preparing to wash up the breakfast dishes. Of Claude Noulton there was neither sight nor sound; presumably he had already departed for the sawmill. The daughter, Rosalee, was seated at the round kitchen table in her work uniform with a mirror propped up in front of her, about to start the process of pinning up her long, lustrous hair. Her green eyes too widened at the sight of the major's pallid face and her lips parted questioningly.

Sommerlott dropped into the chair opposite hers and said flatly, "Frank Hitchens is dead."

The two women gasped simultaneously, but the mother spoke first. "Mr. Hitchens- dead? Oh my stars. I just can't believe it. Was he- was he killed by the same person who's been attacking folks all around town? Or was it some sort of accident?"

"There was no accident. He swallowed a bottle of poison."

"Oh sweet Lord. . ."

The questions came tumbling out then, and Sommerlott answered them as best he could, giving an outline of events without dwelling on the morbid details. Finally he reached the end of his narrative and lapsed into reverie, his deep-set eyes more than ever distant and melancholy. Mrs. Noulton, with a shrewd glance at her guest's harried expression, murmured something about work not getting done and took herself off to another part of the house. Rose, having pushed the last hairpin into place, put the mirror aside and reached across to lay her hand atop the major's. He smiled gratefully at her, and for a time there was the palliation of silence.

Later there were voices at the front of the house and footsteps, and shortly the sheriff appeared in the kitchen doorway, his face weary. He cleared his throat self-consciously and nodded vaguely toward the table. Rose pulled away from the major and started to rise, assuming that the two men would want to be alone to talk, but Sommerlott caught her hand in his and squeezed it in a wordless plea, not releasing it until she had resumed her seat. Talmadge settled into the chair between theirs and dropped his hat on the table next to the major's.

"The whole thing just seems incredible to me," he said. "A man like Frank Hitchens, a pillar of the community- and a cold-blooded killer at the same time. And he took his own life in his own kitchen when he was confronted about it. I don't s'pose there's any chance of this being some kind of colossal mistake?. . . No, I don't reckon there is at that.

"Well, Major, just how'd you come to cipher out he was the killer? Before today I'd've said it was the most fool notion I'd ever heard of. All the facts seemed to point to Jube Inglethorpe, far as I could see, or at least Inglethorpe working with an accomplice. But this. . ."

"I'll try to start at the beginning," Sommerlott said. "Of course you and I were aware from the first that the murderer drove a blue automobile, but that could have fit any number of men. What was of particular interest to me was Crawford Gow's statement about the man he saw entering Perry duBree's home on the evening of his murder. He described the man as going directly to the back of the house before turning on any lights. As you pointed out, the intruder clearly knew what he was looking for. But Mr. Gow's testimony told me more than that: it told me that the intruder, even in the dark, knew his way around the inside of that house, and knew where duBree kept his blackmail materiel. In other words, he'd been inside it before.

"Then there was the fact that Perry duBree's murderer came calling for him at nine o'clock on a weekday morning, which would have meant that he had no regular place of employment at which he needed to be. . ."

"What about the lodge pin we found in duBree's parlor?"

Sommerlott shook his head irritatedly. "I almost feel as if I ought to apologize for ever discovering that confounded pin. All it did was confuse the issue. You recall that I warned you not to put too much stock in it? I found it on the floor directly beneath Perry duBree's hatstand. It was no stretch whatsoever to surmise that it had fallen from one of the articles of clothing above it, especially as a hat with a loose band was among them. What Penny Jewkes told us about his habit of regularly wearing his lodge pin in his hat band cemented my suspicion.

"Although," he added, "you were correct about the murderer being responsible for the pin's presence in duBree's parlor. Mr. Hitchens wore his victim's hat, which had been left behind in his automobile when he disposed of the body, when he entered the house to take away any incriminating papers. No doubt the pin was dislodged when he replaced the hat on the hatstand. He, of course, as you were well aware, had no connection with the Knights of Pythias lodge."

"So were you already on his trail by that point?"

"Not in the slightest. Just then I thought as you did, that the murder was a direct result of Perry duBree's blackmail activities. Marcel Carr seemed to be the most likely candidate for the role of assassin, especially in view of what Mattie Armstrong had to say. He was one of duBree's victims, he'd visited him at his home on more than one occasion, he had no gainful employment. Of course it later came to light that he also had no vehicle of his own, but it was entirely possible for him to have borrowed someone else's automobile to carry out the attacks.

"And then we found him struck down in his room at Mrs. Brett's, and I had to abandon that theory."

"And that was when you hit on Frank Hitchens as the killer?"

"I felt that it was a possibility, but I was hardly certain. Penny Jewkes had mentioned that he had visited duBree at his home, but then duBree might well have had any number of other visitors in the evenings when she wasn't there. Too, Mr. Hitchens was on the scene when Marcel Carr was murdered, but the mere fact of his being a businessman in what is after all quite a small community might have been all the connection there was between those circumstances.

"Actually, the military photograph I saw hanging on the wall of Carr's room started my mind along a different track entirely. Perry duBree and Marcel Carr had belonged to the same Army squad during the War. When I saw that Burton Armstrong had belonged to that squad as well, I found myself asking, What if Mattie Armstrong had been shot by mistake? What if the murderer had taken him for his uncle? The two of them are roughly the same height and build, as well as having the same color of hair, and young Mattie had been standing with his back to the road and a hat on his head when he was shot. If my supposition was correct, then it was conceivable that the murders had nothing to do with Perry duBree's blackmail schemes, that the motive behind them was something we knew nothing about. Was it possible that someone was pursuing a vendetta against the survivors of a particular Army squad? I obtained a list of the survivors of the original incarnation of duBree's squad and set Cole Grayson the task of finding out.

"It was quickly apparent that there was a definite pattern developing along those lines. But if that were indeed the motive, the murderer might well have been someone we didn't suspect, perhaps even someone you and I had never heard mention of. It wasn't until the death of Fred Sears yesterday morning that I knew for a certainty who the murderer was. Do you remember what Mr. Grayson told us when he made his report yesterday evening? Fred Sears, he said, had returned from the War terribly disfigured and had lived a recluse from that time onward, only occasionally venturing from his apartment and never once having visitors there.

"Who, then, could he have possibly known well enough to admit to his apartment, his sanctum sanctorum as it were, except a *fellow member of his old Army squad*?

"It all pointed to Frank Hitchens then. Hitchens owned a blue Essex Coach; the list compiled by your deputy showed that. He had been to Perry duBree's home at least once. As the chief stockholder of several stores on the square he was his own master, free to call upon someone at nine o'clock on a weekday morning if he were so inclined. He had no need of money, even with these straitened times, and so it wouldn't have occurred to him to empty Perry duBree's wallet after he killed him, as it might have a poorer man. He was a member of the same Army squad as the victims, and he was present at Mrs. Brett's boardinghouse when Marcel Carr died."

"That's where I don't follow you, Major. I agree he was on the scene around the time of the killing, but when he went upstairs to Carr's room with Mrs. Brett Carr was already dead. Or wasn't he?"

"He was. But who told us that Mr. Hitchens had only just then arrived? He did. Mrs. Brett thought so as well, of course, but only because he'd done a quick about-face on the stairs when he saw her coming in order to give her that impression." Sommerlott related Hitchens' account of killing Marcel Carr and of locking Carr's door behind him afterward.

"I see." Talmadge stared at the tabletop for a moment, then slanted his eyes at the other man "Major, did he give you any idea at all of his reasons for going after his old Army squad? What did he hope to gain by it?"

Sommerlott, in view of the company, gave the sheriff a brief outline of the killings at Camp Jackson in 1917 and Hitchens' claim that he was bringing a long-delayed justice to the perpetrators.

"I have my doubts, though, as to whether that was really his prime motivation. When I spoke with him on Sunday evening he described his plans for running for county commissioner in the next election, and surely he had ambitions beyond that. It is true, those killings in 1917 were probably not something the authorities would ever have bothered to prosecute, either then or now, but leaving aside any supposed desire for justice, just imagine the wreck that could have been made of his political ambitions if the full details of the incident had been dragged into the open. I suspect the actual motive behind these murders was to ensure the silence of his former comrades."

"Could be, at that. Could be. And maybe you'd care to explain, too, just where this comes in?" Talmadge reached into his pocket and brought out the soiled, tattered ribbon of cloth Sommerlott had left in the dead man's kitchen. "Not that I don't have a pretty fair idea what it means already. . ."

"Ah. Yes, that's the necktie Frank Hitchens was wearing the day he murdered Judd Scott. Scott tore at it in his death throes, leaving blue and purple threads underneath his fingernails and linking Hitchens solidly to the crime. Knowing that Mr. Hitchens would be eager to dispose of such incriminating evidence, and remembering how quickly he had acted to rid himself of his first victim's hat, I sent Cole Grayson along there late last night to hunt for it. He found it at the bottom of the trash barrel at the back of their property, where I'd suggested it would be." Sommerlott shook his head. "That was nothing more than a lucky guess, plain and simple. Hitchens could just as easily have disposed of it in any of a hundred different places, and we would never have found it."

"But you did. And after everything, after all his scheming, to end it all by drinking poison like that. . ."

"That was hardly his original intention," Sommerlott said drily. "It was only when he saw you at his door and realized that it was over, that he was trapped, that he took the poison himself. His burgeoning political career was at an end before it had even begun, so why not end his life as well, and spare himself the scandal and humiliation of an arrest and a trial?

"I was a fool to confront him the way I did, alone, imagining that we could talk the matter over like gentlemen. As far as he knew I was the only one who could connect him to these murders. I haven't the least doubt that if it hadn't been for your timely arrival that poison would very shortly have been in my cup, and it would have been me on the undertaker's table now instead of Frank Hitchens. Oh, he would have concocted a very plausible story to explain my death, I can promise you. . ."

Rosalee Noulton paled noticeably, her freckles standing out against her white cheeks. The major, his gaze turned inward, thumped his fist on the table.

"Imbecile that I was, not to assume that a man who'd already killed six times would have no hesitation about dealing with my interference as well!"

"Major, you expect too much of yourself," Talmadge replied. "Nobody can think of everything. There's no way you could've known he'd be ready and waiting for your visit with a bottle of corrosive sublimate. Come to that, this plan to poison you must've been a last-minute maneuver of his. I s'pose you 'phoned him 'round the same time you 'phoned me this morning, and that couldn't't've given him much time to lay his hands on the stuff. . ."

"Actually, I went directly to the Hitchens home after I telephoned you, and arrived unannounced. Mr. Hitchens had no inkling that I was coming. I suspect he procured that bottle of poison some time ago, perhaps immediately after he learned that his attempt on Burton Armstrong's life had failed. For him to feel that his past was safely buried every survivor of his old squad had to die, but he had no chance of personally carrying out that last murder with his victim sequestered at the Armstrong farm, and Eb Olsen on guard duty with a shotgun. Instead I imagine that he'd devised a strategy to poison Armstrong at a distance, and was only waiting for the right moment to put it into action when I called on him.

"To think that I let myself be lulled by his social standing- a respected businessman, a member of the town council, a devoted congregant. . ."

Rose reached across and laid her hand atop his still-clenched fist, and he lifted his eyes to hers with a faint, crooked smile.

"As the old Latin proverb has it, 'Stultorum infinitus est numerus.'[1] I'm very much afraid, after this debacle, that I must bow my head and admit myself among that fraternity."

"Well, I can't say I know a thing about Latin," Talmadge returned, "but I do know this much- one way or another, these killings are over and done with. And that's what matters."

He pushed himself to his feet, tipped his hat gallantly to Rose and went out, leaving the two of them alone.

---

[1] "The number of fools is infinite."